I0552445

The Mouse and Elephant's Awkward Dilemma

Book Three of The Mouse and Elephant Trilogy

MARK PIPER

The Mouse and Elephant's Awkward Dilemma
Copyright 2021 by Mark Piper

No part of this publication may be reproduced,
distributed or transmitted in any form or by any
means, including photocopying, recording or other
electronic or mechanical methods, without the
prior written permission of the author, except in
the case of brief quotations embodied in critical
reviews and certain other non-commercial uses
permitted by copyright law.

ISBN
978-1-7775459-2-5 (Paperback)
978-1-7775459-4-9 (Hardcover)
978-1-7775459-3-2 (eBook)

Foreword by

Rudy Ghouliani,
personal lawyer for Donald J. Trimp

November 7, 2020

RE: Notice of Intent to File Lawsuit

Dear Mr. Mark Piper,

This letter of intent to sue shall serve as a formal notice that **Rudolph Ghouliani**, LLB, acting on behalf of his client, **Donald J. Trimp, 45th POTUS**, intends to commence a lawsuit against you due for defamation, slander, and unauthorized use of the Trimp name in a series of books filled with slanderous lies and malicious intent.

I. **The Plaintiff: Donald J. Trimp,** CEO Trimp Inc & 45th POTUS.

II. **The Defendant: Mark Piper**, author of *The Mouse and Elephant Trilogy.*

III. **Damage Caused By The Defendant:** *The Mouse and Elephant* series of books has caused catastrophic defamatory harm to **Donald J. Trimp's** previously unsullied reputation; decreased the respect, regard, and confidence in which **Donald J. Trimp** is held by his loyal subjects; and induced disparaging, hostile, or disagreeable opinions or feelings against **Donald J. Trimp** among traitors to the Republic.

Furthermore, our legal team considers *The Mouse and Elephant Trilogy* as the main reason **Donald J. Trimp** was cheated out of the election in 2020. Prior to this series of books *'people were saying'* that **Donald J. Trimp** was the greatest president in history.

IV. **Relief**: As a result of your actions, the Plaintiff seeks relief in the form of:

Seven hundred million US dollars ($700,000,000.00) which shall be used by the Plaintiff to regain his rightful position as POTUS in perpetuity. (Not Canadian money, it's funny looking, worthless, and smells like marijuana or lumberjack sweat.)

V. **Settlement Demand**: You may settle this matter outside of court and avoid a lawsuit by doing the following within 30 days of receiving this Letter of Intent: Paying the total sum of **seven hundred million**

US dollars ($700,000,000) in cash, to the Plaintiff or the Plaintiff's attorney at the Four Seasons Total Lawn Care and Press Conference Head Quarters, 1165 Patriots Way, North Philadelphia (Between the dildo shop and the crematorium.)

V. Governing Law: This Letter of Intent shall be governed under the laws of the State of Florida. Due to the defamation caused by the Defendant, my client is no longer able to visit or conduct legal proceedings in New York.

Sincerely,

Rudolph Ghouliani. LLB

Personal legal counsel for **Donald J. Trimp**

Preface

The Mouse and Elephant's Awkward Dilemma

Book Three of The Mouse and Elephant Trilogy

Mr. Ghouliani, thank you for this. The function of a foreword in a book is to have a famous person or an expert in a specific field lend credibility to the author's work. Therefore, your 'Letter of Intent' is perfect and will provide tremendous value. I'm honoured that you and Donald J. Trimp care enough about my work to consider me worthy of a lawsuit.

I started writing this series in 2015. When I finished the first draft of book one I realised something was missing: an antagonist. I was going to invent a villain - the books are fiction after all - but then Donald Trimp put his name in the Republican Primary. As we all know now, the rest is history. Mr. Trimp has served as the perfect villain or antagonist throughout this series of books.

History and clinical psychologists will not judge Trimp kindly. I wrote these books as a warning: I didn't want to be right. Nevertheless, I'm glad I leaned forward and predicted he'd be a monster before he actually proved it to us. I'm not clairvoyant: these weren't difficult predictions. Donald Trimp has always been a hideous person. It was unlikely the presidency would change him. Sane Americans breathed a sigh of relief when it became clear that Trimp would be a one-term president. So if Trimp is truly gone, why write this book now? Has the danger not passed? Democracy appears to have survived him and dodged his clumsy attempts at becoming king, for the time being at least. I wrote this book because the bigger and more ominous question for future generations is: who will take his place?

You see, Trimp isn't the disease: he's merely a symptom. Trimp's rise to power is a symptom of the metastasizing cancerous hatred, ignorance, and toxicity he ignited among his followers. He made it cool to be stupid, and led a race to the bottom where education was ridiculed and ignorance embraced. The 74 million people who find his despicable views refreshing are the terrifying disease.

The Mouse and Elephant's Awkward Dilemma leans forward and offers a survival guide, a vaccine, and a cure for the near future when those people who worship Trimp find their new Messiah.

Oh, by the way: please don't forget this is a work of speculative fiction. Characters in this story resembling real-life people are purely coincidental.

Mark Piper
5 November 2020

Table of Contents

CHAPTER 1.

We Did Everything We Could...

13 Nov 2020.

Washington

"On Veterans Day, on Arlington's sacred ground, a faction of the KKK murdered 67 people."

The press conference fell silent. "Their target was President-elect Oobima and her husband. In light of that assassination attempt on the Oobimas, I'm recommending that President-elect Michelle Oobima and her staff and family should occupy the White House as soon as possible." The journalists were buzzing like a beehive, hands up all over the room.

During Donald Trimp's presidency, press conferences had gradually dwindled in frequency. Near the end of his administration, there were none. Interim President Nancy

Pillosi brought them back into practice shortly after Trimp and Pens were imprisoned in April 2020.

"In anticipation of your questions," she continued quietly, "we understand that normally, the president-elect does not occupy the White House until after the inauguration ceremony in January. Again, I reiterate that the recent attempt on President-elect Oobima's life should make us consider breaking with tradition. The White House is easier to protect, and it's been empty since Trimp's arrest. Yes, Mr. Hanratty?" she nodded at the Fox News senior reporter.

"Ms. Pillosi, why do you consistently disrespect President Trimp by referring to him as simply 'Trimp'? Aren't former presidents still entitled to be called president after their term?"

"Mr. Hanratty: we've answered this question many times," President Pillosi responded acidly. "Trimp has been found guilty of serious crimes against our country. I don't believe former presidents who have committed crimes against our country are entitled to ongoing respect. Next question. Yes, Julia?

"M'am why didn't you move into the White House following Trimp's arrest?"

"I'm an interim president," she replied softly. "I'm the president because our forefathers were smart enough to include contingency plans in our Constitution if the president and vice president were unable to fulfill their duties. The person occupying the president's official residency should be elected, not appointed during a crisis."

In an era when many politicians were loud, rude, and bombastic, Nancy Pillosi was like a grade four teacher from the fifties. Indeed, her own Grade four teacher from the fifties, Miss Brown, was her model or inspiration when addressing the public. She could shout when necessary, but she saved her shouting voice for rare occasions. It was pointless to shout all the time.

"I cannot and will not shout all day," Miss Brown quietly told her students. "When I am speaking, you must be quiet and listen carefully to me. If you cannot abide by these rules, then you must leave my class, and discuss your behaviour with Principal Gilinski."

President Pillosi nodded at a CNN reporter. "Jim?"

"Ma'am, are there any updates on former President Barack Oobima?"

***

This is the worst part of my job, Dr. Phu thought... *I hate losing any patient but ...* The 2nd child of Vietnamese immigrants, she was the youngest resident to ever graduate from Johns Hopkins medical program. Her peers at the Walter Reed Medical Center unanimously regarded her as the top emergency surgeon in the capital district, if not the whole country.

"Time of death, 01:54," Dr. Phu stated grimly to her team in surgery. "Close up the deceased, advise the morgue, and prep this OR for our next patient," she told her team.

She took off her gloves and surgical mask, drew a deep breath, and opened the door where the Oobima family and their security team were waiting nervously.

"Madam President," she began. "I'm Dr. Phu. I'm so sorry. We did everything we could, but..."

Her explanation went unfinished. Malia and Sasha rushed to Michelle Oobima, who struggled to stand, turned very pale, staggered, and looked ready to faint. The girls embraced their mother and cried quietly together for a minute.

"I'll leave you alone for now," Dr. Phu stated, "but if you have any questions, I'm here for you at your convenience." As she turned to leave, Michelle Oobima stood and willed herself to speak.

"Dr. Phu, I need to say.....thank you for your efforts over the past 36 hours. I know that you and your team did everything that you could for my husband."

"We did indeed Madam President."

"Dr. Phu, I want to see my husband's body and speak to your team before he leaves the operating room."

"Madam, we don't allow this. It's not standard procedure. You could see your husband in the morgue after an autopsy has been conducted."

"Dr. Phu, as the president-elect of the United States, we're going to make an exception in this case. It's important to me," Michelle concluded with a note of finality. "Girls, I'll only be a minute, please wait here." Malia and Sasha had been getting up, but they recognised the tone in their mother's voice.

"Stephen, I'll do this alone, thank you."

Stephen Smith's response was firm but polite. "I'm sorry Madam President. We all have our orders. Mine state that the president never goes anywhere unescorted. Ever. No exceptions."

Michelle sighed, then nodded. '*Even presidents don't get to do what they want all the time*' her husband used to joke. *Used to joke,* she thought sadly, holding back more tears.

Dr. Phu reluctantly led the way, with President Oobima and her security detail close behind.

"Ladies and gentlemen, we have a special guest," Dr. Phu announced quietly as the entourage entered the OR. Barack Oobima's body had just been closed up. This was no place for the squeamish.

" I'll try to make this quick," President Oobima began. She spoke with surprising clarity and poise considering the circumstances. Michelle was physically wiped out. She hadn't slept in 48 hours. She had lost two fingers and now her husband in an assassination attempt on their lives. "I know that you are busy. But I needed to take a minute to thank you for your efforts: today, last week, last year, yesterday, tomorrow...." She looked around the room as she spoke, making eye contact with the ER team. For their part, the doctors and nurses silently nodded their appreciation.

"Dr. Phu, how many times was my husband shot, and what was the nature of the resulting wounds?" she asked in a clinical voice, moving closer to her husband's corpse.

The young surgeon drew a deep breath, hesitated, then noted the determined look in Michelle's eyes and responded. "Your husband was struck by 13 rounds Madam President," Dr. Phu replied, illustrating with a laser pointer. "Once here in the left forearm, and once here in the left thigh, which badly damaged the femoral artery. The other 11 rounds were, unfortunately, all in the thoracic cavity, which irreparably damaged his heart, both lungs, his liver, his spleen, a kidney, his bladder... Two of the rounds also hit the spine, which caused severe nerve damage. Madam, we could have repaired one or two of these injuries, but the injuries to so many major organs were too catastrophic to repair. I'm sorry we couldn't do more."

"Dr. Phu, I know that you did all that you could. Thank you for letting me see my husband, this was important to me."

Michelle nodded to Stephen Smith. "Let's go home." The Oobima family were hustled into their car by the ever-present security detail. Most of its members were new. Stephen Smith and part of tonight's shift had been on a rare day off when the Arlington attack occurred. That recent attack on President-elect Oobima and her husband had claimed 67 lives. 11 of those lives were assigned to the Oobimas security detail. The new replacements were still in shock: shock at losing their friends and comrades in arms, shock at their sudden promotions, shock at...everything that had happened recently.

The presidential motorcade was rolling back to the White House, with Michelle, Malia, and Sasha crying quietly together in the back seat of an up-armored limo. "Momma, this is awful," Malia sobbed through angry tears. "Can we just walk away from all this, this... bullshit?" She waved her hand, encircling the motorcade, to illustrate the mad circus that presidents and their families must endure. "I mean, our father and all those other innocent people were murdered, you're injured, and I don't think these haters will stop until we're all dead." Malia broke into fresh tears, crying so hard she was gasping for breath.

In response, Michelle Oobima hugged her girls tighter. "Shhhhh. Sweethearts. I can't undo what's done. I know you're upset and sad, and angry, and scared, and of course, we're gonna miss your father, and, yes, what happened was awful. But if your father was still here, do you know what he'd tell us?"

"Some lame Dad joke?" Sasha sniffed through her tears.

Michelle smiled sadly. "Probably. But then he'd tell us that we need to persevere, and fight the good fight, and never, ever give up. If we give up now, the bad guys win."

The motorcade was passing through security gates at the rear of the White House. Malia and Sasha had lived here for eight years: longer than in any other home they'd known. As the Oobimas stepped out of the car, their dogs, Boo and Sunshine bounded out to meet them. Michelle looked quizzically at Stephen Smith. "How did they get here?"

"Same way everything else did Ma'am. In the last 24 hours, we've moved all your personal effects from your private residence back into the White House. These two insisted on coming with us." Stephen paused to shake the dog's paws and resisted the urge to provide the belly rubs the two were clearly begging for by rolling on their backs.

The White House Staff was up and waiting for the Oobima's. Just one of the faces- the old chef, Jeremiah Jackson- was familiar from when the Oobima's had lived here previously. Many of the staff from 2016 had quit or been replaced by Trimp in 2017. When Nancy Pillosi was appointed interim president in 2020 she had replaced many of Trimp's appointees. "Many of these people were vastly unqualified to serve in their positions," Pillosi said simply. "Most were friends of Trimp or children of friends of Trimp."

Rachel Maddox, the new Press Secretary, and Dwain John-Stone, the new Vice President huddled quickly and quietly with Michelle.

"No," Michelle shook her head at the new VP. "I'll tell them."

To Maddox, she added quietly, "I'll need you to draft a press release for me."

She stepped forward and cleared her throat to address the assembled staff. "Thank you for being here for us, especially on such short notice. I'm sure over time, we'll get to know each other better. For now, I wish I had better news, but you should be the first to know." She paused briefly, then plunged in.

"My husband, my soul mate, the father of these two wonderful girls, and the love of my life is gone." She was searching for more words, but they wouldn't come, nor were they required. The White House staff, following Jeremiah Jackson's lead, wrapped the Oobima family in tearful embraces for the next few minutes.

The new White House doctor was a tall Navy commander named Susan Love. Nancy Pillosi had appointed her when she took over as interim president. Doctor Love had seen more than her share of shock and trauma in her 22 years of service. She had served in MASH hospitals in Iraq, and Afghanistan, and had deployed aboard the hospital ships USS Comfort and Mercy on disaster relief. What she saw now was a very tired president who had campaigned tirelessly for a year, been shot two days ago, and had witnessed countless others dying in a hail of bullets. Since the attack, she hadn't left her husband's side, nor slept. *And now her husband is dead,* Dr. Love thought to herself. "We need to let the president get some rest," she said quietly to Vice President Dwain John-Stone. The Stone nodded in agreement.

"All right folks," the commander stated. "I'm sorry. I know we are all hurting right now, but let's allow our president and her family some time to rest." The White House staff quietly broke away from the Oobima family, leaving Michelle and her two daughters looking alone, vulnerable, ashen. The staff were visibly shaken by the news of the former president's death. The doctor, Malia, and Sasha quietly thanked the last few staffers as they drifted away from the president.

"Madam President, ladies. I'm Dr. Love. Ma'am, I want to change the dressing on your hand. Ladies if you could come with us to your mother's room please." The commander led the way.

Michelle hadn't slept in more than 48 hours. It was obvious. Michelle Oobima fell asleep in a bedside chair while the doctor worked quickly and efficiently to change the dressing on her hand. She spoke quietly to Malia and Sasha as she worked, explaining that the wound was healing well. "Nevertheless, I'm giving your mother an injection that will reduce the chance of infection, promote healing, and help her rest. Now, let's get your Mom changed and ready for bed, yes?"

"We got this part doctor, thanks," Malia said.

"Can I help you with her?" the doctor asked.

"Thanks, Ma'am, but we got this," Sasha responded.

"We're stronger than we look," Malia added.

"I never doubted it," the commander said, quietly closing the door behind her.

***

CHAPTER 2.

That Can't Happen Here...

Ottawa

OMG, how tough are women? Elijah thought for the hundredth time, fighting the urge to faint as Juliette screamed through her pain. He was torn between watching his young wife suffer through childbirth and marvelling at the doctor's skill.

It hadn't been an easy delivery for Juliette Sparks. Her water had broken more than 18 hours ago. After what seemed like an eternity of never-ending labour pain, her babies were apparently racing to see who could be born first. To complicate matters further, the first baby trying to exit was in a breech position. The obstetrician was using forceps to try and turn baby number one into a better position to exit the birth canal. Baby number two had tried to thwart the obstetrician by bear-hugging baby number one.

"Almost there Juliette, the first baby is crowning, give us a big push now," the doctor encouraged. "Look Dad, a beautiful head of curly hair." Elijah watched, wide-eyed, wordless, as their daughter won the race to be born first. Her younger brother followed a few minutes later. "Congratulations Mom and Dad, you've got two healthy happy babies," the doctor told the elated couple.

A few moments later, Juliette was somehow miraculously beaming, radiant, majestic, holding both her newborn children. "Juliette: you've never looked more beautiful than you do right now," Elijah told her through tears of joy.

"You've all had a very long day," the doctor told Elijah and Juliette after a suitable time had passed. "We need to run a few standard tests on your new babies. Juliette, we're going to give you some intravenous fluids to avoid dehydration and check you over, and then all of you - babies included- would benefit from some sleep."

"Do they need to be fed?" Juliette asked anxiously.

"Not right away," the doctor replied. "Maybe in a couple of hours? Your babies will let us know when they're hungry, and we'll bring them to you." Two nurses whisked the babies away efficiently, pausing to let Juliette and Elijah kiss each precious newborn child. Another two nurses were holding the curtain around Juliette's bed expectantly. "Sir, if you can, uh, give us the room."

Elijah took the hint and kissed Juliette. "Get some sleep," she told him sternly. "It's 4 AM. And you look wiped out."

"I feel wiped out," he responded honestly, backing slowly out of the room. "But how is it you did all the hard painful work, and still look absolutely fabulous?" he responded, through a closing curtain.

His young wife laughed from behind the curtain. "Have you still not figured this out? Girls are soooooo much tougher than boys."

"Have you picked the babies' names yet?" a CBC journalist asked Elijah on the steps outside the Ottawa hospital.

"Sir: a boy and a girl? Is that correct?" another reporter shouted over the scrum.

"Yes. A boy and a girl," Elijah responded. "My beautiful wife and our new babies are happy and healthy." More questions were shouted. "Yes we have picked names, but I need to speak with someone before that news is public. Maybe by tomorrow, yeah? But right now, I'm really tired, and I gotta get some sleep. Excuse me." His security detail hustled him into a black sedan that had just rolled up.

The story of the young hip Canadian prime minister and his popular cabinet minister wife having twins was a momentary blip of happy, hopeful news for a world far too accustomed to sad and violent news stories.

That small glimmer of hope and happiness didn't last long.

"Sir, I'm sorry to disturb you, but there is something you need to see." Elijah had just fallen asleep. A large man wearing a turban was shaking him gently. Lateef was a plainclothes RCMP officer assigned to the prime minister's security detail. Elijah checked his watch. *It's 0530,* he thought to himself. He held up two fingers to Lateef and stumbled to the bathroom. Two other RCMP security officers were waiting with Lateef. "Two minutes," he stammered. He peed, brushed his teeth, and washed his face with cold water. "It's 0530," he told himself again, looking in the mirror.

"Sorry, Sir. This just happened." The younger of the two officers began to brief Elijah. An hour later the story broke.

"This is a CBC News Special Report. Viewers are warned that the following report is graphic in nature, and contains hate speech and violent images that many will find unsettling. Minister of Foreign Affairs Dustin Trudel and 2 security personnel are reported as dead following a rocket attack moments ago near the nation's capital." The image on the screen showed a smoldering black diplomatic limousine, upside down, surrounded by police cars and emergency vehicles.

"The former Canadian prime minister was en route to the Ottawa airport when the attack occurred," CBC anchor Ian Manohansing intoned gravely. "Trudel had been scheduled to speak at the Washington Press Club dinner, and later in the week at the funeral of former U.S. President Barack Oobima. The cowardly attack leaves the three Trudel children without a father," Manohansing continued. "A far-right white supremacy faction known as 'Ku Klux Kanada' have claimed credit for the attack. Again, I'll warn our viewers that this message is vicious hate speech, it is graphic and vile. Normally, the CBC would not show a message of this nature; however, the group claiming responsibility for this murder has already released the message via social media." The message rolled on the screen, with a swastika on the top and bottom of the page.

'Pay attention Snowflakes.

Trudel deserved to die.

He was a weakling, a champion for all you 'triggered' whiners worldwide.

His death should serve as a warning to libtards and socialists everywhere.

Trudel poisoned our gene pool by bringing in millions of filthy immigrants.

He gave away billions of our tax dollars to stupid lazy foreigners in shit hole countries.

He crippled our economy with ridiculous carbon taxes.

Trudel was a symbol for everything that is wrong in Canada today.

Like-minded left-leaning, snowflake socialists everywhere should heed this warning.

We are the Master Race.

Your 'Resistance' is futile and pathetic.
White Power!'

***

Niagara Falls Ontario

Cpl 'Lumpy' Halerewich, Pte Fabiola Gonzalez, and two other militia soldiers were assisting the Royal Canadian Mounted Police. They were outside a rusty old sea container on a flatbed trailer. The trailer was parked in a muddy gravel lot by a crumbling warehouse on the wrong side of the tracks. They were wearing white disposable coveralls, latex gloves, and surgical masks. It was 0615, and bitterly cold. An RCMP sergeant was briefing them.

"First, I want to thank you for volunteering for this detail. What you are going to see inside this sea container is not pleasant," she stated point-blank. "You'll work with Constable Blake. Our forensic analysts have swept the crime scene, but we may find other evidence as we proceed. Don't rush. Move slowly, cautiously, deliberately. Keep your PPE- your personal protective equipment - on at all times.

If you feel overwhelmed, or anxious, or like you're gonna be sick, let Blake know." As she spoke, another tractor-trailer with a refrigerated box pulled into the muddy parking lot and backed up to a side door on the seacan. RCMP officers cloaked the area between the two trucks with tarps to void people seeing in. Meanwhile, more officers and militia soldiers were taping off and guarding the perimeter of the warehouse and parking lot. When the reefer truck was in place, the Sgt nodded at Blake. "Let's get started."

Steps were leading up to the seacan. "These are slippery," Blake told the soldiers. "Use the handrail." The morning sun was just rising, but inside the seacan was very dark. Once inside, Constable Blake flipped a breaker. Lights on tripods had been set up, powered by a generator humming outside. The soldiers gasped at the scene inside. The seacan was full of dead people.

Pte Fabiola Gonzales looked around the room in horror. Many of the victims wore clothing made from textiles produced in her home country of Guatemala. *Madre Maria: these are my countrymen* she began to pray silently, blinking through her tears as she listened to Constable Blake's instructions.

"Our job is to get these corpses into body bags, and into this reefer truck. The reefer truck is going to be the morgue for this case, our county morgue isn't big enough to process these numbers. We'll start here, nearest the door," Blake directed. "This corpse has already been tagged as number one." Corpse one was a young man, *maybe 20? my age?* Fabiola wondered.

"So - first- you lay out the body bag here, and open it," Blake directed, pointing at Lumpy and Fabiola. "Now, you take the feet, and you take the torso. On my count of three, you're gonna lift together and put the body on top of the open bag. Ready? One, two, three, lift."

The two soldiers laid the young man's body on top of the body bag. "Now, see, how the corpse is stiff from rigor mortis?" Blake asked. Fabiola and Lumpy nodded mutely. "So I need you to press the legs down flat," Blake told Fabiola, "and I need you to push the arms down flat," he told Lumpy, "or we won't be able to close and carry the body bag. On three- firmly now- one, two, three, push." Fabiola prayed silently through tears as she worked. Some air gurgled from the deceased man's lungs as they straightened out the limbs. It was the kind of sound you can't forget if you've ever been unlucky enough to have heard it.

Lumpy got up quickly, pulled down his mask, walked two steps, and vomited on the floor. "I'm sorry," he gasped, trying to catch his breath between retches.

"It's alright," Blake told him quietly. "That's a normal reaction to an abnormal situation. Put the rest of that in here if you can." The constable slid a garbage can under the young soldier and handed him some paper towel to clean himself up. He opened a bag of cat litter and covered Lumpy's deposit on the floor. This was not Constable Blake's first rodeo. "You take a minute and catch your breath: we're gonna close up this bag, and put the bag in the reefer truck. You OK?"

"Yeah, thanks. I'm alright now."

"Alright- stay here- just watch what we do, we'll be right back." Blake pointed at Fabiola. "Now, you close up the bag from bottom to top, that's it, very good. We're gonna lift again on three, ready?" Blake and Fabiola carried body bag # 1 into the refrigerated truck that was serving as a temporary on-site morgue.

"OK," Constable Blake said as he returned to the group. "There are 34 more corpses. You two," he pointed to Fabiola and Lumpy, "stay with me. And you two," he pointed at the other two soldiers, "go with Constable Wong up at the front of the seacan. Like the Sgt said outside: don't rush. Follow our instructions, and we should be done here in about one hour."

***

Ottawa

Elijah was clearly exhausted. It was obvious to his Cabinet. The ministers had been summoned to an emergency meeting at 0900. Drawing on reserves he didn't know he had, the young prime minister somehow willed himself forward. "In the past 72 hours, the world has been horribly shaken," he began. "Former President Barrack Oobima and 67 other innocent people were murdered in cold blood on Veterans day in Arlington Virginia. This morning, Dustin Trudel, our former prime minister and minister of Foreign Affairs, and 2 of his security detail were assassinated while en route to President Oobima's funeral." Elijah paused briefly to look at his ministers. The cabinet ministers were aware of Trudel's very recent assassination, but still reeling from the shock of hearing it.

Elijah drew another deep breath and plunged on. "I'm sorry, I know this sucks, but I have more bad news. The RCMP just briefed us on a terrible case in Niagara Falls. 35 Guatemalans trying to immigrate to Canada have been found dead in a sea container in Niagara Falls. The early report indicates that the same group who murdered Dustin is taking credit for this mass execution as well. The Cabinet Ministers were shocked, horrified, weeping, or struck silent staring at the floor. "I'm with you right now," Elijah continued, crying, fighting for breath through his tears. "I'm terrified. I'm angry. I'm embarrassed for our country and incredibly sad. But right now we need to put our emotions on hold. Right now we need to act quickly and decisively. We don't have the time right now to be emotional. That is not a luxury we can afford. Right now we need to lead. The floor is open. Please help me. Don't hold back."

Elijah didn't have to wait long. Harjit Singh had been deployed on three occasions to Afghanistan as a battalion commander in the reserve. When he wasn't deployed or training with the army, he had been a police officer leading an anti-drug task team in Vancouver. He had seen more than his share of horrible things, and understood that leaders needed to put personal emotions on hold and lead in times like these. He'd been elected as a member of parliament in 2015, and appointed as Minister of Defence shortly thereafter.

"I recommend we implement the Emergencies Act immediately," the minister said solemnly, rising as he spoke. Heads around the room nodded in quiet assent. "Our first order of business must be to protect our citizens. The Emergencies Act allows us to do this. We could pass this through parliament this morning. The Chief of Defence Staff has kept an up to date plan for troop deployment across Canada, as we have had the concern of civil unrest ever since Trimp's imprisonment. Unfortunately, it appears that Trimp's message of hate has been embraced here. Those haters are now acting. The Emergencies Act will give us the security needed to protect Canadians from further violent crimes, and give police forces broader powers of arrest of persons we believe may be responsible."

Several hours later, the Emergencies Act was passed in the House of Commons. It was the most sombre meeting of MPs assembled in recent history. The members of parliament left the chamber and headed back to their offices. Danni Grey Eyes and Benjamin Big Canoe had become Elijah's closest friends. Benjamin wrapped an arm around Elijah as they walked to the PM's office.

"My brother, you need to get some rest," Benjamin Big Canoe whispered to Elijah.

Elijah did look exhausted. "I know, I'm wiped out," he replied weakly. "But I can't sleep right now. I'm scared, I'm angry, I'm confused." He seemed lost for words, which was rare for Elijah.

He sat at his desk for a moment, then brightened a bit. "I'm a new father." Danni and Benjamin smiled at their friend. "I'm a new father," Elijah repeated. The three were hugging and crying happy tears when Less Izmore and Charley Shackleton came into the office. Charley was wearing his customary coveralls, workboots, and an old tweed jacket that smelled like a barnyard. Good barnyard though: not nasty barnyard.

A journalist from the *New York Times* recently wrote "I visited Charley Shackleton - Canada's Minister of Agriculture- at his family farm in Springfield, Ontario. Spending a few hours with Charley and his dog Fred makes you want to curl up under a blanket in a rocking chair by a woodstove with a cat in your lap, and a dog at your feet. He is a living breathing character from a Norman Rockwell painting, and one of the most unusual political figures in the world."

Charley had a bottle of good Canadian rye whiskey and five old fashioned glasses in a box. Without speaking, he put the glasses on Elijah's desk and poured a stiff shot into each glass.

"Charley, you know I don't..."

"I know you don't usually drink," Charley interrupted in a slow drawl. "Just humour me. It's not every day a man becomes a father." He pushed a glass towards Elijah with a big calloused mitt and passed a glass to the others. "To the twins," he toasted, raising a glass.

"To the twins," the other four responded. Elijah gasped as the whiskey burned its way down his throat.

"Have you and Juliette picked out names yet?"

"How is she doing?'

"The baby's are healthy?"

"Are Juliette's parents here now?"

"And your parents?"

Charley quietly refilled glasses once more as the group fired questions at Elijah quicker than he could answer.

There was a quick knock on the door, and Elijah's assistant MoneyPenney entered the room. If she was surprised to see a bottle of whiskey on Elijah's desk, she didn't show it. "Sir, apologies for the interruption. You requested that I arrange a call with the president of the United States? I've got her here on line one. Are you able to take the call here?"

"Yes, of course," Elijah responded. "Put her through. And you guys stay right here," he said to the cabinet ministers, who were getting up to leave. Elijah had called President-elect Oobima to congratulate her on the night of the election. It seemed so long ago. He reminded himself that only eight days had passed. He punched a button on the phone. "Madam President, this is Elijah. Thank you for taking my call. Do you mind if I put you on speakerphone? I have four of our cabinet ministers here with me."

"That would be fine Mister Prime Minister. May I do the same? I'm with Vice President John-Stone."

"Of course, but please call me Elijah. It's just our small group here. We're pretty informal."

"OK, but only if you call me Michelle."

"OK, Michelle it is," Elijah responded. "Michelle: I wanted to call and offer you condolences, from our whole country, on the loss of your husband. Please, please let us know if there's anything we can do to help you get through this."

"Elijah, we appreciate that. And I in turn want to offer our condolences to you on behalf of Dustin Trudel: this was shocking news. Barack and I and our girls just adored

Dustin and his young family. Should I call Sophia?' Is it too soon?"

"It's never too soon to comfort a friend. I think she'd love to hear from you." Elijah took a sip from his glass, grimaced at Charley, and pressed on. "Michelle, I know these are dark sad days for both of us, but I wanted to let you know a few things personally, so you aren't just hearing it on the news."

He briefed the president-elect quickly on his concerns regarding the right-wing fanatics who had killed former Prime Minister Trudel, and almost simultaneously, the Guatemalan refugees. Michelle Oobima had not yet heard the news regarding the refugees, and Elijah explained that it had just happened. They briefly discussed how their police forces could cooperate to quell this latest hideous outburst of fanatic violence. He went on to explain that Canada's parliament had just passed the Emergencies Act, and what effect that would have on border crossings.

Elijah continued speaking. "Madam President, pardon me; Michelle. This has been an awful few days for both of us. We've both suffered some terrible losses here. Both of our countries are under attack from some very evil people. Personally, I've never been more concerned about our two countries than I am right now. I speak for a lot of Canadians when I say that we are horrified, and shocked, and deeply, deeply saddened by what's happened to all of us in the past week. I want to end this call with a ray of sunshine, or happy news if I may?"

"I think we could all use some good news, Elijah. Please."

Elijah smiled dryly. "Juliette and I are the proud parents of two new babies, a boy, and a girl."

"Whoop Whoop!" 'The Stone' shouted in the background.

"Elijah, I'm so happy for you and Juliette," Michelle said. "Please forgive me, it's been so, uh, chaotic here I'd forgotten you two were expecting."

"Michelle; there is no need to apologise after what you've been through. But I want to ask you a favour though?"

"Ask away."

"Ma'am, with your permission, we'd like to name our children Michelle and Barrack?" Elijah asked hopefully.

The line from Washington was silent for a minute.

"Hey, Elijah: This is Dwain," the Vice President boomed. "President Oobima says she'd be honoured, and she thanks you for this. Listen brother: I know we're all busy. Congratulations on Michelle and Barrack. I'm looking forward to meeting them, and to helping make their world a safer and happier place. We'll speak again soon, yes?"

"Indeed we will. Please convey our thanks to the president from Juliette and myself."

"I will," 'The Stone' promised. "Hasta luego."

The room in Ottawa was quiet for a minute.

"To Barrack and Michelle!" Charley Shackleton stood and toasted quietly. The other 4 joined him thoughtfully, reverently. "To Barrack and Michelle!"

Charley and Less Izmore gathered up the glasses and left the office quietly. Benjamin and Danni both hugged Elijah, and with an arm around each shoulder, helped him gently to the couch in his office. Elijah tried to resist. "I can't sleep now," he said through tears to his friends. "There is so much to do, I need to ..." He looked frantic, anxious, frightened.

"You must sleep," Danni Grey Eyes told him gently. "We need you rested. Your new family needs you rested. Ben and I will shake you in a couple hours."

The two friends covered him with a blanket and dimmed the office lights on the way out.

***

CHAPTER 3.

Don't Drop Your Soap...

And we're rolling on camera two in 3, 2, 1, Action!

"This is Fox Nation. I have bad news for all you whiny outraged snowflake liberals out there. I'm still standing, and I'm still Tommi Lauren!" the blonde newscaster announced confidently to Fox viewers. "Today the Fox network proudly announces *'The Apprentice: Leavenworth'* is coming to Fox TV this December. Producer Mark Brunette who produced the original record-breaking reality series *'The Apprentice'* starring Donald Trimp, in 2004, is with me now. Mark: good morning, and congratulations."

"It's a pleasure, Tommi. We're really excited about this latest series of *'The Apprentice: Leavenworth'*" Brunette responded.

"I know the public is excited to see our favourite President, Donald Trimp, back in our living rooms," Tommi gushed. "We understand that there were and still are many challenges in bringing this reality show back to television?"

"Yes, indeed. Our first challenge was in getting any access at all to a federal penitentiary with our television crews. Interim President Pillosi and her administration tried every underhanded trick in their crooked lawbooks to deny Mr. Trimp and the viewing public this opportunity. But Tommi, as you know, President Trimp only hires the best lawyers." Mr. Brunette paused briefly as the cameras switched from two over to three.

"President Trimp himself convinced the warden and the attorney general that this show could do many wonderful things to help educate the public about our criminal justice system and improve its effectiveness. First, the public should know that Mr. Trimp has generously agreed to donate his entire salary of 16 million dollars, to his new foundation called 'Third Chances'."

"Pardon me Mark, but President Trimp just keeps giving and giving and giving, despite all the horrible and unfair treatment he's endured," Tommi Lauren interjected. She could not contain her enthusiasm or admiration for her president any longer. "First he donates his presidential salary to charities, and now this. Have you ever met a more generous and kind-hearted man?"

"Honestly no Tommi. I can't think of anyone else who's given so freely of himself to America," Brunette replied.

"And as you said, it's more remarkable when you consider how unjustly he's been treated by the radical left who want to destroy him and all his tremendous recent achievements as president."

"Mark, please tell our viewers: how is President Trimp doing? Is he being well treated? Is he safe?"

"Tommi, President Trimp is an incredibly strong man. His mental and physical health is exceptional, and he and the warden and the other prisoners are all getting along tremendously. He is tutoring business classes for other prisoners- again, for free - he's teaching prisoners with literacy issues to read and write. But you don't have to take my word for it, Tommi. I can show you a sneak peek from episode one if you like. We'll let President Trimp himself tell our loyal Fox viewers how he's doing."

Tommi Lauren was beaming. "Another Fox exclusive: President Trimp's first message directly to Americans after his unjust incarceration! We'll be back, right after this word from our sponsor, the National Rifle Association!"

"... and cut!" Tommi's producer was jacked right up. "Tommi, Mr. Brunette: that was fabulous. We are making history here." He chattered away happily, while the makeup team applied powder to take the shine off his star host and her guest.

Sadly, it was true. Anything Trimp did or said since 2016 was like a train wreck: people had to look and listen. How could you not? The staunchest Never Trimpers still couldn't avoid watching him. When asked why 78 % of people polled said "morbid curiosity I guess? He's a lunatic and a convicted criminal who somehow became our president?" The other 22% said they still watched, listened to, and revered President Trimp "because he's the greatest president our country ever had, and God will smite his enemies. President Trimp will MAGA again, you'll see!"

Or words to that effect.

Todd Nugent, the lead guitarist of the Motor City Mudmen, and current NRA president was wrapping up his commercial for people to join the National Rifle Association. Membership was at historic lows, and 'many people were saying' the association was teetering on bankruptcy.

"American patriots," Nugent shouted, "our way of life, our sacred Second Amendment rights to bear arms given to us by God are under attack from evil socialists. Now, more than ever before, your membership in the National Rifle Association is essential. Michelle Oobima and Nancy Pillosi will take our guns and enslave us in socialism!" The commercial ended with actors who closely resembled President-elect Oobima and interim President Pillosi lighting a pile of guns on fire using a copy of the Second Amendment as the fire starter.

"Tommi: we're back on in 3, 2, 1, Action..."

"This is Fox Nation: welcome back. I'm still Tommi Lauren. Our guest today is Mark Brunette, producer of *'The Apprentice'* and *'The Apprentice: Leavenworth'*. Mr. Brunette, congratulations on this new show. Now, I can't wait any longer. Just before the commercial break, you told us we can have a sneak peek of *'The Apprentice: Leavenworth?'"*

"Promise made, promise kept, Ms. Lauren. Ladies and gentlemen, I present to you President Donald J. Trimp." Brunette smiled graciously, as the footage rolled.

"Hello, America. It's me, your favorite president, here in Leavenworth, starring in *'The Apprentice: Leavenworth.'"* The former president of the United States was seated at a cafeteria table in the Leavenworth cafeteria, surrounded by other well behaved and earnest-looking prisoners. As the cameras panned in closer, the most observant viewers noted that the inmate number on his orange prison coveralls was 45.

"First: I want to thank my loyal supporters: your thoughts and prayers, and generous donations to the Trimp Foundation have allowed me to stay strong during these dark times. As you know, there was no collusion or quid pro quo. And it was the perfect call, I mean, perfect. And I never touched that woman. But, Crooked Mallory Clifton and Lyin, Cryin Nancy Pillosi, and all those shifty pencil-necked socialists in the 'Deep State' have managed to impeach and imprison your favorite president for crimes

I didn't commit." His fellow inmates looked sad or angry at the injustice being done to their new friend.

The cameras panned out further as Trimp continued speaking. "But that's OK, America. I've made new friends, there are some wonderful wonderful people here in Leavenworth, on both sides. The men we'll feature on *'The Apprentice: Leavenworth'* are great guys, who really do deserve a third chance." As Trimp continued speaking, the inmates gathered around him, arms folded, looking like they were willing to repent for their sins.

"I'll be teaching them some literary skills, reading, writing, I know words, I mean, I have the best words," Trimp rambled. "I went to the best schools, I made top of my class, dean's list at Wharton. Listen America: here's the important part," Trimp paused and made that gesture he always made to let Trimpamzees know to listen closely, the index finger on the thumb thing. "I'm innocent, and I'm coming back to MAGA some more. But until then, I'm gonna help these men get ready for life outside. Did I ever tell you I'm really rich? It's true. I mean, I'm so rich, Rudy says we can't even calculate how rich I am. That's why I donated all my presidential salary to charity. and, it's why I'm going to donate 16 million dollars, all my salary from..."

Trimp was interrupted at this point by the inmates who applauded wildly, and then began to chant "Lock Her Up! Lock Her Up!" The irony of this was apparently lost on

Trimp, who smiled that goofy smile that he wore at his hate rallies whenever the crowd got this out of their system. After a minute, he calmed the inmates down and resumed speaking. "Like I was saying, I'm so rich, I'm gonna donate my entire salary of 16 million dollars from this show to my new charity 'Third Chances.' And all that money will go to help REAL Americans, like these men, not pinkos or globalists or socialists."

"God bless you President Trimp!" the biggest, most dangerous looking inmate shouted. The inmates surrounded Trimp, almost group hug like but carefully not touching his hair. They'd been briefed.

"America: Tune in next week to see: *'The Apprentice: Leavenworth.'*" Trimp shouted into the camera. He and his new co-stars gave his famous 'two thumbs up' pose and smiled. The trailer faded out with Old Glory waving in the background.

Tommi Lauren was wiping away tears. "Honestly Mr. Brunette, I mean, how does this man remain so gracious and humble despite all the injustices and transgressions against him?" Mark Brunette appeared ready to answer, but the producer was waving his hands at Tommi in a 'cut' motion. "I'm sorry, Mark, we need a minute. We'll be right back after this word from our sponsor, Monsanto."

***

CHAPTER 4.

A Time to Mourn and A Time to Dance

Washington

Throughout that November, most Canadians and Americans were re-united in grief, shock, and horror. Although the two countries had always shared a special relationship, Trimp's reign of greed and hatred had seriously strained those bonds of friendship and mutual respect. The Oobima and Trudel assassinations and subsequent state funerals reminded citizens in both countries of their many similarities.

Both are comparatively young nations. Both nations were built by immigrants on land stolen from indigenous persons who are still being marginalised. The two nations share the world's longest border. They are each other's largest trading partners. Many Americans have family in

Canada, and vice versa. Both countries are blessed with abundant natural resources and vast geography.

Before Trimp, Canadians would never comment on the political choices their American neighbours made. That all changed when Trimp began to make executive decisions that served to enrich the wealthiest while damaging the natural environment the two countries shared.

November was a blur for Elijah and Juliette. The proud new parents brought Michelle and Barrack home to the prime minister's official residence on 24 Sussex three days after the twins were born. Juliette's mother Portia flew in from Halifax to live with them for a while and lend a hand. Elijah spent one evening at home with his newborns and left the next morning on official business.

Elijah was one of many world leaders who flew to Washington to attend Barrack Oobima's funeral. The Pope was there. So was Bono, 65 prime ministers or presidents, JayZee, Bayonce, Queen Elizabeth, and Queen Latifah. There were three eulogists, chosen by Michelle Oobima and Nancy Pillosi. Nancy had wisely recommended that the three speakers discuss their eulogies amongst themselves, to avoid repetition, and not 'steal the other's thunder.'

George 'Dubya' Busch, who had become an unlikely friend and ally to the Oobimas spoke first. President Busch was a better speaker than people gave him credit for. He dryly joked that it was more easily done when not being crushed under the weight of the presidency. He spoke on how well Barack Oobima had met 'the difficult challenge of leadership with humanity and dignity.'

President Busch was followed by Ayanna Priestly, a young congresswoman from the Independent People's Party. She spoke of how Barack Oobima had inspired millions of young people around the world with messages of hope and examples of courage. Her electrifying hypnotizing eulogy of Oobima put her on the 'shortlist' of young people with a legitimate shot at being the next president of the United States.

Elijah was the only foreign dignitary to speak during the service.

He delivered the speech that Dustin Trudel had written, a day before Trudel himself was assassinated. The fact that Elijah had named his newborn children after Barrack and Michelle was not lost on people. Trudel's speech, delivered by Elijah, was beautifully simple and heartfelt. The fact that the man who wrote it had been assassinated the next day in a hate crime only served to elevate its historical significance.

"My dear friend Dustin Trudel wrote this for his dear friend and ally, President Barrack Oobima. I'm doubly heartbroken that Dustin can't be with us today to share this with you," Elijah began, looking at the Oobimas, fighting to keep his emotions in check.

"I know hearts are breaking right now. Please remember this: the night is always darkest just before the dawn. Our good friend Barrack would ask that we use this sad occasion to raise our game, to grow as people, to be better to each other, to help a friend who is feeling down, to reach out to someone who has never agreed with us, to forgive those who have trespassed against us."

Elijah, much like Barrack Oobima, was a gifted speaker. It was on full display during this eulogy for Barack Oobima in the Washington National Cathedral. Some people speak too quickly or don't pause in the right places to let our brains process what we just heard. That pause is essential for us to feel an emotion about what was just said. A good speaker can make us feel as though they are speaking to us individually. With a look or a glance in the right direction, or the proper inflection, by quickening or slowing the cadence of their words, by raising or lowering the volume of what is being said, they can somehow reach us. It's a gift. Martin Luther King had it. John F. Kennedy had it. Barack and Michelle Oobima, Winston Churchill, and Elijah had it.

"Michelle, Malia, Sasha: as a young father and recently married man, I always drew inspiration from spending time with Barack. He showed Sofia and I that no matter how busy we are, no matter how important we think our jobs are, no matter how frantic and hectic our world has become, despite all this pressure, the most important thing we need to do is to be good to our families, be good to ourselves, simply be decent and kind to people: these are the most important things we can do in life.

When Sophia and I first went to Washington on our first state visit with our young family, I was overwhelmed and terrified. I was a newly elected prime minister, meeting the leader of the most powerful nation on earth. There was so much to be done, so many people to meet. Barrack Oobima instantly calmed all my fears and anxiety. You all met us coming off the plane. Malia and Sasha, you became big sisters and role models to Xanadu, Estelle, and Eugenie. You showed them that in spite of their Dad's unusual job, it was okay to just be a kid. Thank you for that kindness, we'll never forget it.

Michelle, you formed an immediate bond with Sophia. Your husband, Barack, had a wonderful perspective on all of this and told me how he always set aside time for you and your two girls. On our first state visit to Washington, rather than being rushed off to some high profile international meeting, your family took us to the White House. Imagine this if you can: Barack Oobima barbecued chicken and ribs for us." The assembled congregation in the cathedral chuckled. They could see it.

"Malia and Sasha: you two young ladies played with our kids, your dogs got to play fetch with all of us. We were simply two families, spending time with each other. It was one of the most memorable days of my life. Your

Dad told me something that day while we watched you playing with our children. He said: *'Dustin, I'm inspired by the people I meet in my travels-hearing their stories, seeing the hardships they overcome, their fundamental optimism and decency. I'm inspired by the love people have for their children. And I'm inspired by my own children, how full they make my heart. They make me want to work to make the world a little bit better. And they make me want to be a better man.'"*

A screen behind Elijah had been showing pictures while he spoke. Pictures of Malia and Sasha meeting the Trudel kids. Pictures of Barack and Dustin Trudel in shirtsleeves smiling over a grill. Pictures of Michelle and Sophia laughing and beaming with pride while teaching Malia how to hold a newborn Eugenie. The images kept coming. Barack Oobima holding twins. Visiting wounded soldiers. Eulogizing John McClain, his long time political rival who was also a close friend. Greeting children at the White House for Halloween, Christmas, and Easter. Consoling parents in Sandy Hook. Hugging George H. W. Busch when Barbara passed. Consoling the Busch family when their father passed. Laying on the floor of the oval office with a newborn child. The pictures rolled on in the background.

"Barack: you taught us all to be decent, to be kind, to protect the helpless, to uplift the downtrodden. You taught us to always hope. Normally, in a eulogy, we hear quotes from a famous historic figure who inspires us. I want to leave you with several of my favorite quotes from a man loved dearly by hundreds of millions of people worldwide. He was a poet laureate for his generation. His name was Barack Oobima. He told us that *'Change will not come if we wait for some other person, or if we wait for some other time. We are the ones we've been waiting for. We are the change that we seek.'*"

Elijah drew a deep breath. "We are living in a dangerous time right now. We shouldn't have to be here today. Our friend Barack Oobima was a decent, generous, kind man. He gave his life in service to his country. Going forward, let's remember what he told us at Senator John McClain's funeral. He told us: *'There's not a liberal America and a conservative America - there's only the United States of America.'*"

"May God bless Barack Oobima, and may God bless these United States of America."

After the service, President Oobima's flag-draped coffin, accompanied by an honor guard was scheduled to travel on a funeral train to lay in state all 48 contiguous state capitols. The funeral train was a tradition begun for Lincoln's funeral and was most recently used for George H.W. Busch Sr.

***

Ottawa

Dustin Trudel's casket (his remains were cremated) had lain in state in the centre block of parliament for three days. Many of the same international leaders of nations who had attended Oobimas funeral were present. The celebrity list was somewhat different. The Pope attended and sat with leaders from nine other religions, including the Aga Khan, the Archbishops of Canterbury, and the Eastern Orthodox Churches, and the Dalai Lama. Queen Latifah didn't know the Trudel's, but Queen Elizabeth was there, as were 24 of the most senior leaders of the Assembly of First Nations in their traditional dress.

Five days after her own husband's funeral, Michelle Oobima spoke at Dustin Trudel's funeral in Notre Dame Basilica in Montreal. Malia and Sasha had made the trip with her. Keen students of history and those with long memories recalled that Dustin Trudel had delivered his own father's eulogy in the same cathedral. Many Canadians believe Dustin's eulogy for his father launched his political career.

Michelle Oobima's eulogy was beautifully written and delivered. She highlighted Dustin's tremendous contributions to diversity, to the environment, to indigenous persons, to women's rights, to world peace, to immigrants. Even people who didn't like the Oobimas grudgingly admitted she displayed tremendous dignity, strength, poise, and grace under very arduous circumstances.

Elijah delivered the second eulogy. He and Juliette had been among Dustin and Sophia Trudel's closest friends for the past several years. They both had young families. They were both young people when compared to the traditional image of politicians as old white men. Elijah and Dustin Trudel had campaigned against each other in 2019, but neither attacked the other. Quite the opposite in fact: they had tremendous respect for each other. Elijah highlighted the Dustin Trudel that the general public may not have known without meeting him. A good friend, a fun person, a loving person, a sympathetic person, a forgiving person. It was a warm, moving tribute to a friend.

The third eulogist was a tremendous surprise to those watching worldwide. It was none other than Her Royal Highness, Queen Elizabeth the Second, Sovereign of the British Empire and the Commonwealth. She had spoken with Elijah at President Oobima's funeral and offered to deliver a eulogy. Not really offered. Insisted or decreed, Elijah realized.

"Isn't that a bit, umm, unusual, Your Majesty?" Elijah wondered aloud. "I mean, it's not something you would normally do?"

"Quite right prime minister," the tiny Queen replied in her clipped, precise oxford English. "It is highly unusual for a Monarch to speak at such an occasion. Nevertheless, the world is in a frightful state at the moment. When I was a very young woman, long, long ago, I was fortunate enough to have Winston Churchill as my first prime minister."

"That is fortunate," Elijah said.

"Indeed. With time, I came to appreciate his wisdom and guidance. However, at that time I was terrified. I was 27 years old, and Churchill had a well-earned reputation as an awful bully and tyrant. Nevertheless, our first meeting and all meetings subsequent were educational, gratifying, and often, quite humorous. During that first meeting, I asked the prime minister if I should speak at an event that was on our calendar, I can't for the life of me recall what it was, so it cannot have been of tremendous import..." The elderly monarch seemed to drift away for a minute, lost in her memories of days gone by.

Elijah waited patiently.

"Prime minister: aren't you going to ask me what Churchill replied?" she snapped, with a mischievous twinkle. "Do try to keep up."

"Sorry. What was Churchill's reply, Your Majesty?"

"He told me gruffly that *'The Queen should endeavor to speak as little as possible, and the less often, the better.'* I thought this rather rude, and he could see that I thought so. He let me think on this for a moment, and then explained in a softer tone. *'Your Majesty, if the Crown addresses the public too often, the occasion becomes commonplace and lacks significance. We should instead save your public addresses for traditional times, like the Christmas message, and for those dire times when the shit has truly hit the fan.'"* Queen Elizabeth paused for a moment to let this sink in.

"Unfortunately, Mr. Prime Minister, that time is now."

"Your Majesty." Elijah nodded.

Listen to any of the messages that Queen Elizabeth has delivered over her 68 years on the throne. Her words carry tremendous weight. *Churchill was right,* Elijah realised as he listened to her speak. She was like a 94-year-old tiny secret weapon, unleashed for only the most momentous occasions.

She spoke graciously of meeting a precocious Dustin Trudel as a five-year-old when his father Prime Minister Pierre Trudel visited Buckingham Palace. "We met again on a visit to Canada when your father was 13," she said to the Trudel children, "and again on several visits when he had become prime minister. I also very much enjoyed meeting you, Sophia, and your three lovely children, on your last visit to Buckingham Palace. You should know that your father was extremely proud of you, and fiercely devoted to you all. I enjoyed watching him grow up, from a child to a young man, and eventually to devoting his life to the service of your great Dominion of Canada. Be proud of your father," she told the Trudel children warmly. "Carry him always in your hearts, as I shall in mine."

The elderly sovereign shifted focus. Her condemnation of the terrorists who had assassinated a former president and a former prime minister was fire and ice and scorn. Her voice was steel and dripped derision. As she spoke, people saw her strength of character, and realised that this person had survived the Great Depression, the Blitz of London, and served in World War Two.

"I speak now to those of you whose evil actions have brought us here, in this time, at this place. You are the worst sorts of cowards and bullies. We do not fear you in the least. Our great nations have defeated fascists and murderers in the past, and we shall do so again. Your only weapons are hatred and loathing. You lurk in dark places and strike at the unarmed. Over the coming days, you shall be apprehended. You are evil personified. Evil can never conquer the righteous. The remainder of your days will be spent in fear and shame. You shall not know peace or rest. Not in this life, nor in the next."

She changed her tone again, from steel to velvet, and softly laid a gloved hand on the flag-draped coffin. "Prime Minister Trudel, your work here on earth is finished. I have always enjoyed your company. I believe we'll meet again soon."

As the Queen took her seat, the fourth eulogist, stood, kissed his mother and two younger sisters gently, and proceeded to the dais.

"Good morning. My name is Xanadu Trudel. As the oldest child in our family, I wanted to thank all of you for taking the time and making the effort to be with us today. It means a lot to us."

After hearing the Queen speak, Xanadu's voice rang clear like a soprano bell. He was 13 and tall for his age. "My sisters, Estelle and Eugenie, helped me write down some memories of our father we'd like to share with you. Most of you knew him as a politician, some of you knew him as a friend. We knew him as our father. He took us canoeing and camping. He taught us how to start a campfire, and to skate, and to swim. He took us to karate classes and soccer practice."

As the young man spoke, he explained photos and video as this rolled in a screen behind him. Some had been seen before, in newspapers, and on television. Many had not. "This is my Mom and Dad on their wedding day. This is my Dad when he was 13, with his father, meeting Queen Elizabeth in London. That's me and my Dad and Mom in the maternity hospital here. My Mom liked to tease him that he almost fainted when we were being born. That's my grandfather meeting Fidel Castro with my father as a baby in a papoose. This picture shows our Dad reading a bedtime story to Estelle and Eugenie, while Eugenie puts makeup on him. Here's a video of all of us at the White House with the Oobimas. This picture is my father welcoming refugees and their families from Syria. This is a picture of us burying our dog that died last year..."

The young man continued narrating between heavy sobs. It was absolutely heart wrenching. The photos were a warm intimate look into the life of a man most people only knew as a public figure and politician. Xanadu wiped away tears that had been freely streaming down his face. "So that was my Dad. He was 48 years old this year. He spent most of his life honestly trying to help people. My sister Eugenie is six. She wanted me to share this with you."

Xanadu brought a crumpled note from his pocket and opened it. As he read from it, the note appeared on the screen behind him. It was printed as neatly as a six-year old can print.

"To the people who killed my father: that was a mean thing to do, and you've made us very sad. At first, I was mad at you, but my Maman told me you must be sick, cuz you killed people who try to help everyone, like my father. So, if you are sick, please get help, like from a doctor or a teacher, or a priest. So now I'm just sad. I'm not gonna stay mad at you. I forgive you, but please get some help, and don't hurt any more people."

***

CHAPTER 5.

We Have Super Secret Spies?

Ottawa

Most Canadians understood why their government had declared the Emergencies Act in mid-November. 35 people trying to immigrate to Canada had been murdered. Former President Oobima and former Prime Minister Trudel had been assassinated in the same week. Trudel's assassination happened while travelling to the airport to speak at Oobima's funeral. The Canadian and American chapters of the KKK were taking credit for both assassinations and the mass murder of the Guatemalan refugees. There was widespread concern that hate groups in the United States and Canada were working together to terrorize persons of colour, immigrants, and 'liberal snowflakes'. "Yes, the government was right to implement the Emergencies Act," was how 64 percent of Canadians responded in a recent national poll.

Of course, no government can please all of the people all of the time. There was much discussion of what the Emergencies Act allowed the government to do. Social media sites like Twitter and Facebook were filled with articles and discussions on "The Oppressive Danger of Martial Law: Why You Should Be Worried." The same topic was being hotly discussed and debated in coffee shops from Tofino to Twillingate. Naturally, the discussion made it to Question Period on the floor of the Canadian Parliament, where members of parliament ask questions to "seek information from the government and hold it accountable for its actions."

"Please take a moment to understand the difference between martial law and the Emergencies Act," responded Harjit Singh, the Minister of Defence. "Canada has never declared martial law. In our history, we have declared the War Measures Act three times. In 1988, the name of the Act was changed from 'War Measures' to 'Emergencies'. The War Measures Act and the Emergencies Act which replaced it stop short of martial law. The Emergencies Act does temporarily give the Canadian government tremendous powers. It allows the military and police forces to arrest and detain persons suspected of crimes without laying specific charges, without a search warrant, and to detain those persons in order to safeguard Canadian citizens. Those persons arrested under the Emergencies Act may eventually be tried in our courts under normal judicial processes. Martial law is different. Martial law allows the military to try and convict persons accused of crimes in military tribunals or courts-martial. Our parliament recently enacted the Emergencies Act to keep Canadians safe during an emergency. It's not martial law. We have no interest or intent in trying Canadians accused of crimes in military courts-martial."

The discussion was happening because various Canadian police forces, Canada Border Services Agents, and CSIS, all bolstered with Canadian Forces troops, had arrested more than 33,000 people in a four week period.

Wait. What? Who is CSIS? Many Canadians were unaware of the Canadian Security Intelligence Service. "*That's a thing? We have a Security Intelligence Service? And spies?*"

"Yes, we're a thing," replied the CSIS director in a rare TV interview.

"Director, do CSIS, umm, agents, wear a uniform? How would Canadians know if we were talking with a CSIS spy?" the new host of CBC News at Six asked. Heather Jones had just been hired. Ironically, a CSIS agent had recently investigated and ordered the arrest of the former host of News at Six. Heather was blissfully unaware of this. She didn't ask how the door had opened, she was just grateful to step through it.

"We find our operators and analysts do better work when we fly under the radar, and don't advertise who we are," the director responded. "Therefore we don't wear uniforms. There is no clear requirement that CSIS agents disclose that they work for CSIS. As we are a spy agency that primarily conducts covert activities, secrecy is inherently required. Moreover, CSIS often uses informants to secretly obtain information."

"So I may have spoken with a CSIS agent and not been aware of it?" the young journalist asked hopefully. The director often encountered people who hoped for a sexy spy 007 sort of encounter.

"It's possible. Have you been involved in acts of terrorism, the production of weapons of mass destruction, espionage, foreign interference, and cyber-tampering affecting critical Canadian infrastructure?" the director asked sternly.

"No, of course not." She seemed a bit surprised at the question.

"Well, then no, you probably haven't spoken with one of our agents," the director chuckled. He removed a shoe and spoke into it. "Agent 66, abort the mission. Ms. Jones is not a threat."

"What was that? Were you just talking into your shoe?" Heather Jones asked incredulously.

"Agent 66 has been riding in your trunk the past two mornings. We have several means of communication, including the shoe phone."

Heather was lost for words. Momentarily. "You can't be serious."

The director sighed. "Sadly, you're right. I'm not serious. We've been trying for years to perfect the shoe phone, but these Canadian winters play havoc with the electronics." Ms. Jones still looked confused. "I'm sorry. I couldn't resist. I'm just messing with you. I've wanted to use *'the shoe phone'* line for years. Just google *'Maxwell Smart, shoe phone,'*" the director said, shaking his head. "To your viewers under 60, I apologise, my references here are quite dated I'm afraid."

"So there isn't a spy in my trunk?" Heather Jones sounded disappointed.

"Correct. I do want to let your viewers know that Canadians have nothing to fear from their Canadian Security Intelligence Service agents. Unless they're plotting something evil of course."

"Director, thank you for this. I'm sure many Canadians didn't know we had a super-secret spy service here. How exciting!"

"Please, don't get too excited. The reason we are a successful *'super-secret agent'* organization is precisely because very few people know we exist. I should also let your viewers know that we're always looking for suitable personnel. To learn more about us, and the application process, visit CSIS.CA."

The 33,000 arrests in Canada resulted in the seizure of a tremendous amount of illegal weapons. High capacity assault rifles with bump stocks, handguns, millions of rounds of ammunition, sawed-off shotguns, biological agents, anti-tank missiles, nerve gases, artillery pieces, dirty bombs, and similar items. These had all been restricted or prohibited items in Canada for many years of course. The staggering number of seized weapons surprised many Canadians. Gun lovers in America were likewise appalled at the seizure, albeit for different reasons.

Social media sites were filled with posts like: "*You'll be sorry Canuckistan. This is how socialism starts. Here in America, we're clinging to our guns and Bibles! No Guns? No Freedom!*" *#FromMyColdDeadHands!*"

The standard response was often something like:

"Sad but true. You're right. We don't have the freedom to massacre each other with high capacity assault rifles. Oddly enough many of us are good with democratic socialism. I'm pretty certain a lot of us identify as atheists as well. See, up here in Canuckistan, we're pretty weird. We have health care and gun control. We elect politicians who promise to keep it that way. By contrast, you have health control and gun care. Please try to understand the difference. #ThoughtsAndPrayers.

A significant number of cyber terrorists were also arrested while the Emergencies Act was in effect. Their intent was to hack into and cripple or degrade power stations, electrical grids, government sites - including Elections Canada, water treatment plants, banks, credit card companies, universities, and hospitals - to name just a few intended targets.

"Commissioner: who is being arrested under the Emergencies Act?" journalists asked the head of the RCMP at a press conference. "What sorts of crimes do you suspect they have committed?"

"We're arresting terrorists, members of hate groups, drug dealers, thieves, gun smugglers, internet and phone scammers, pimps and human traffickers. In short," the commissioner replied, "we're arresting people who have committed crimes."

"Commissioner, can you define what a hate group is?" a reporter from *The Maple Leaf Post* wondered. "And, is it illegal for Canadians to belong to one?"

Arrrghhhh, not these questions again, thought the commissioner. But she gave the textbook answer. "So, a hate group is an organization, club or social group that advocates and practices hatred, hostility, or violence towards members of a race, ethnicity, religion, gender, sexual orientation or any other designated sector of society."

"So, by that definition, the Royal Canadian Mounted Police were a hate group when they harassed and intimidated you for your gender, colour, and sexual preference?"

"No," she responded quickly. "Definitely not. And I resent the manner in which you framed the question. The RCMP is quite the opposite of a hate group. Look, unfortunately, the RCMP had some members who did not follow our protocol and guidelines regarding equality, diversity, and equal opportunity for all. An investigation was held and those members were disciplined, and training was provided to avoid reoccurrences." Commissioner Talib's case was well known. She was the first female ever selected to head the iconic institution. The fact that she was an openly gay black woman hadn't made it any easier to climb the ladder, especially early in her career. Her complaints of harassment and intimidation, along with complaints from numerous other female officers and persons of colour initiated a country-wide investigation into the Mounties.

"So what's an example of a hate group in Canada?" the reporter persisted.

"Well, the Ku Klux Kanada is the most recent and best-known example." answered the commissioner simply. "Their stated mandate is *'to re-establish white Christians as the master race in Canada.'* If you still aren't convinced, read the letters that the KKK wrote when they claimed responsibility for the murders of Dustin Trudel and 35 Guatemalan refugees."

"So is it illegal to belong to such a group?" another journalist asked.

"Well, the law is many shades of grey regarding that question," Talib responded thoughtfully. "But it is certainly illegal to commit a hate crime. or use hate speech. So if a person belongs to an organization identified as a hate group or terrorist cell, then we have grounds to arrest that person under the Emergencies Act."

"So Canadians don't have free speech anymore?" the most persistent journalist asked. "Isn't this how fascism begins?" *The Maple Leaf Post* is like an online Canadian version of *Breitbart* sprinkled with Alex Janes.

"See now you're just being silly," the commissioner replied curtly. "Canada's Constitution protects freedom of expression, but it also protects multiculturalism and equality. I'll give you two examples of how that works. You could publish an article that says you don't approve of me as Commissioner because I'm incompetent, or lazy, or stupid. That's OK, and that is your opinion. But if you wrote an article that said I shouldn't be the Commissioner because I'm gay, black or female, now we have a problem." The journalist was now looking at his feet, blushing and slightly embarrassed, but Commissioner Talib wasn't finished. "If you wrote that all persons of colour, or all women, or all gay people are incompetent, lazy, or stupid, that's not OK. Our Criminal Code in Canada says a hate crime is committed against a group of people rather than a person. Do you see the difference? When a person or persons are attacked for who they are, rather than what they've done, we have a possible hate crime." Commissioner Talib paused to catch her breath and to glare at the reporter. "Any other questions for me today?"

***

Niagara Falls

The Niagara Falls Regiment, like all Canadian units, were extremely busy while the Emergencies Act was in effect. The Regiment was deployed to the four bridges: Whirlpool, Lewiston- Queenston, Rainbow, and Peace. Those bridges lead to the United States, most within 30 kilometres of Buffalo, New York. Their mandate was to provide extra security, an extra level of screening, and to augment the Canada Border Services Agents employed there.

Sgt. Maj. Michelle Lee had deployed on three occasions: twice to Kandahar and once to Iraq. Each of her deployments was nine months long.

Warrant Officer Turnbull knocked on her office door. "Sergeant Major, 223 troops in the theatre ready for you."

"Thanks, Warrant. Let's go." Sgt. Maj. Lee led the way. The theatre was buzzing with chatter from the soldiers seated side by side. Most were young. The average age of the Regiment was 21. 43 members of the Niagara's were still completing Basic Training within the unit. Sgt. Maj. Lee strode smartly to the dais, halted, and executed a smart turn to face her troops. The chatter diminished but didn't stop entirely.

"SHUT YOUR PIE HOLES, MAGGOTS!" she shouted, with a voice that cracked like a pistol. The room went immediately silent and sat to attention: spines erect, both feet on the floor, head and eyes level and straight ahead, shoulders back, arms in, thumbs in line with the seam of the trousers. She looked around the room disdainfully for a moment, then smiled sweetly. "Relax." She nodded at Turnbull, who closed the door. "You know, I don't enjoy calling you maggots," she continued. "But when you behave like maggots, then it is my job to correct your maggoty shortcomings. In the future, one way to avoid maggoty behaviour in a situation like this is for one of the senior persons in the room to call out ROOM when a person of higher rank enters or leaves the room. Then all of the persons in the room sit or stand to attention, and cease to chatter." She looked at the sergeants in the room briefly. They withered slightly. "It saves us all a lot of time," she said quietly. "BECAUSE YOU'RE NOT REALLY MAGGOTS ARE YOU?" she shouted. People were always amazed that such a tiny person had such a powerful voice.

"NO SERGEANT MAJOR!" The room responded as one.

"Today we will discuss our upcoming role in support of our Border Services Agents. Our role at the border is going to be important. We'll be doing vehicle and personal searches. Do this wrong, and someone dies. Do it right, and you possibly save lives. The first part of this brief is death by PowerPoint. Stay awake, stay silent. If you have a question, raise your hand. After this brief, we will break up into your squads, and we will practise the Standard Operating Procedures for vehicle and personal searches.

***

Ottawa

Canada's recently expanded military was based on a formula that had worked well in two World Wars. In 1914 and 1939 Canadians had expanded the military rapidly, and organised their army on the British system. After winning the election, Elijah's IPP government wanted to expand the military again. Quickly. The Indies (as the Independent People's Party had been nicknamed) implemented conscription that required each Canadian under 25 to serve for one year in some capacity, and for two weeks per year thereafter until 60 years of age. The two week period of service each year was to maintain hands-on training and skills in common requirements like first aid, small arms, fire fighting, and military occupation-specific training on new equipment or procedures.

"We are not at war, and there is no threat of war," various opponents of the Independent People's Party had shouted in parliament. "This is a ridiculous proposal that we cannot afford."

"The Honourable Members are partially correct," Elijah responded calmly. "Canada is not at war in the traditional sense that we are not under attack by an invading force, nor do we see the need to attack another nation in the near future. Our intent is to employ our military members in peacetime roles: for disaster relief at home and abroad, in peacekeeping, in public works, in aid to the civil power, and as climate change warriors to environmental threats."

The Militia Act offered those not wishing to serve two options. The first was a two-year prison sentence. "Option one is a shitty choice," Elijah told Canadians. "We're still going to put you to work on public projects in prison, but you're not going to be paid much."

Option two was perhaps even more unpopular than option one. "Citizen's not wishing to serve may opt-out with a onetime payment of $100,000.00 to the Receiver General and subsequent annual payments of $5,000.00 per year till age 60."

"Both options are despicable," shouted those in opposition. "Option one forces poor people to join the military or go to jail. Option two allows the wealthy and privileged to avoid this *'mandatory period of national service'* painlessly."

"Incorrect," the defence minister responded. "Option two is not painless at all. A person 20 years of age will pay a total of $325,000.00 by age 60 to avoid their period of service. Our government will use that money to pay the wages of those persons serving in our reserve forces. I would not call that painless at all."

Criticism of options one or two for conscription avoidance was soon forgotten. Very few people elected for either option. "What the fudge, it's only a year," a lot of young people rationalised. "The money is okay, I get to play with some cool equipment, I'm training with other people my age, I feel like I'm doing something useful, and giving back to my country."

***

Niagara Falls

Cpl Lumpy Halerewich initially didn't want to join the militia. He was one of the first people in Niagara Falls to get a conscription letter after Canadians elected an Independent government. The day he was supposed to enrol, he didn't show up at the Armory in Niagara Falls. The Military Police picked him up, he spent one night in cells and decided that maybe the militia was worth a shot. By the end of the first day, he was having fun. Lumpy was a straight-up grunt, an infantry soldier. When his anniversary date for release drew close, he asked to stay and was given a three-year contract.

The Niagara Regiment, like many across the country, consisted of:

> nine soldiers per Squad;
> three Squads in a Platoon (30 soldiers);
> four Platoons in a Company; (120 soldiers);
> two Companies in a Battalion; (250 soldiers); and
> four Battalions in a Regiment. (1000 soldiers).

The Niagara Regiment was made up of number one Battalion from Niagara Falls, numbers two and three from Ste Catherines, and number four from Stony Creek. Generally speaking, an organization like this promoted friendly competition and healthy rivalry: between Squads, Platoons, Companies, Battalions, and Regiments. The troops knew each other and competed against each other at each level. Each group wanted to be the fastest, strongest, or smartest. "Or at least, not the slowest and stupidest!" Lumpy had famously yelled at his squad after they got lost during a Regimental exercise a few weeks back.

"Beginning tomorrow morning, our Battalion will work at Rainbow Bridge," Sgt. Maj. Lee explained, pointing at a diagram at the front of the theatre. "The Fourth from Stony Creek....*jeers hoots, catcalls* will be at Peace Bridge. St. Kates number two ...*more jeers and whistles* will be at

Lewiston-Queenston Bridge, and St. Kates number three... *bwahahahahaha* will be at Whirlpool Bridge." Sgt. Maj. Lee checked her watch. "Your company commanders will brief you next: Bravo Company, you'll be staying here in the front part of the theatre. Alpha Company, you'll be in the back. After the commander's brief each company, we'll practise vehicle and personnel searches. Cpl Halerewich: have four of your best and brightest pull that sliding partition."

Lumpy snapped to attention. "Sergeant Major!" Lumpy replied.

Cpl Halerewich was the corporal of three squad, two platoon, Alpha Company. Each squad had six privates privates, one corporal, one master-corporal, and one sergeant. Three squads of nine soldiers each made up a platoon of 27 soldiers lead by a warrant officer, a lieutenant, and a captain for a total of 30 soldiers per platoon. The four platoons in Alpha Company trained as infantry soldiers.

Lumpy's girlfriend Fabiola Gonzalez was a private in two squad, one platoon, Bravo Company. Bravo Company trained in communications and intelligence operations. Fabiola was an Intelligence Operator. Her additional language skills in Spanish and K'iche (an indigenous Mayan language spoken in Guatemala) had been called into service recently. She'd been helping the RCMP with the murder investigation of 35 refugees from her homeland.

"Our number one Battalion is quite a diverse group," their commander was bragging to his peers at a Regimental Dinner. "We have soldiers able to communicate in 16 languages: English, French, Mandarin, Farsi, Spanish, K'iche, Ojibwe, Polish, Italian, Bengali, Gaelic, Croatian, German, Flemish, Swahili, and Portuguese."

"Sir, I've been meaning to update you on this topic," Sgt. Maj. Lee interjected. "I believe our new number is 18 languages now."

"We have some new troops, Sergeant Major?"

"No sir. But the Padre's been holding out on us. In his initial interview, Father Jakub told us he speaks English and Polish." Father Jakub began to blush, fearing the worst.

"Yes. Does he speak other languages?"

"Yes Sir, he does. Last weekend he got into the krupnik with some of our troops at Gramma Hanna's boarding house and was later heard speaking in tongues... *BWAHAHAHAHA...* Sgt. Maj. Lee gave the crowd a minute.

"and then the next day at Mass he was speaking Latin..." *BWAHAHAHAHAHAHAHA.*

***

CHAPTER 6.

The Audacity of Hope

Washington DC

"President Oobima: what do you hope to achieve in your first term as president?" a reporter from The Guardian asked her.

"Hope," she responded quickly. "I love that word. I hope that we can learn to hope again."

People worldwide seemed keen to join Americans in celebrating their first female president, their first independent president. Globally, it seemed like the dawn of a brave new era in American politics. Her administration was putting tremendous effort and energy into healing a divided nation. Figurative olive branches of all sorts were extended but were often returned covered in bile or feces, dripping with hate. They weren't real olive branches of course, nor was the bile and feces. At least not in most cases. Let's just say the staff in the White House mailroom were using a lot more gloves and biohazard suits than ever before.

The x-ray scanners and metal detectors could pick up the obviously dangerous items: crude pipe bombs, IEDs, and so forth. The dogs were good at detecting some of the other items. One of the White House interns started a list. There were all sorts of boxes filled with various kinds of human waste, and lots of dead animals, most the victims of roadkill. Possums were a popular Christmas or inauguration gift to the new president. There were a few porcupines, cats, and loads of catfish, carp, and flattened frogs and toads. Most were accompanied by a letter, wishing Michelle and her family glad tidings and best wishes.

Just kidding.

There were so many security threats directed at President Oobima that the FBI, CIA, and her Secret Service team were overwhelmed. "Madam President: we can't guarantee your safety, or public safety if we do your inauguration at the National Mall. We need to be able to restrict and reduce the crowd size significantly to minimize the threat."

"No. We will not govern our country from behind a shield," she replied quickly. "I have every faith in our security services, and your ability to pull this off safely from The Mall." She stood up. "This is what the haters want. They want us to be afraid, and to hide. We will not give in to fear. We will not hide. Take what steps you feel necessary to keep the public safe, but the inauguration will take place on the National Mall, as has been the recent custom."

***

President Oobima's trust in her security services was rewarded with a reasonably peaceful inauguration. The crowd was pro-Michelle, younger than most, and larger than any in history. The perimeter of the site for a five-mile radius around the National Mall and the Capitol buildings was already being monitored with two types of electro-optic surveillance systems: both a long-range system and a short-range day and night system.

The public wishing to attend had to fill out an application for pre-screening 21 days before the inauguration. Those persons who passed the initial screening were sent an acceptance letter and a bar code number to be shown at the first checkpoint. Those who did not pass the pre-screening were sent an explanation of why they were being refused entry. Some of those persons were also visited by various police forces and arrested.

Those persons who got an acceptance letter still waited for six hours to get through three increasingly detailed security checks. The first checkpoint was a verification of the acceptance letter, identity, and a pat-down body search. Each person was tagged with a button that had to remain visible and had a tracker assigned to the person's barcode. The button could only be removed by security personnel at the exit points.

The ID attached to that person's button was transmitted to the second checkpoint, where that person was screened again for threat potential, patted down again, checked by security dogs, and passing through a backscatter X-Ray machine.

The third checkpoint included passing through a screening area to check for gas chromatography and a metal detector. Security personnel arrested more than a thousand people that day. Most were arrested at the first checkpoint, 43 at the second checkpoint, and two at the final checkpoint. The weapons confiscated included: guns made of metal, wood, glass, plastic, and potatoes? Knives of glass, wood, metal, leather, bone, crucifixes, stone and antler, several prosthetic limbs altered to serve as weapons or bombs, several persons who had bombs surgically implanted by backyard doctors. Wineskins, fake colostomy bags, and water bottles filled with gas, napalm, and various acids. Molotov cocktails of all sorts, several suicide vests, and, a man posing as a blind priest who surgically implanted a bomb inside his guide dog. (The 'priest' was arrested, and the bomb was successfully removed from the guide dog.)

The inauguration itself followed the standard script. First, 'The Stone', Dwain John-Stone was sworn in as Vice President by the Chief Justice of the Supreme Court. Next, Michelle Oobima was sworn in as the 47th POTUS. (Don't forget, Nancy Pillosi had been the 46th POTUS, following Trimp's and Pens' arrests. Die-hard Republicans certainly hadn't forgotten.)

Presidents and vice presidents often took their oath of office with their right hand on a Bible, opened to a favorite scripture. Those keenly interested in inaugural trivia (like Fox News) noted that Vice President John-Stone had his hand on the Book of Revelations, Chapter 13, Verse five.

"And there was given unto him (the beast) a mouth speaking great things and blasphemies and authority was given unto him to continue forty and two months."

Evangelical Republicans were furious. "Are you suggesting that Donald Trimp was *'the beast?'*"

"Oh, I'm not suggesting that at all," 'The Stone' replied in a Fox interview, trademark eyebrow raised. "I just find it interesting that the Bible was able to predict that we would have a man like Donald Trimp in office for forty-two months."

President Oobima's verse was more well known and well-received. She asked the crowd at the inauguration to recite it along with her.

> *"Our Father who art in Heaven, hallowed be thy name.*
> *Thy kingdom comes, thy will be done on earth,*
> *as it is in heaven.*
> *Give us this day our daily bread.*
> *And forgive us our trespasses, as we forgive those who*
> *trespass against us.*
> *Lead us not into temptation but deliver us from evil:*
> *For thine is the kingdom, and the power, and the glory.*
> *forever and ever,*
> *Amen."*

It is a powerful prayer. It sounds truly amazing when recited by two million three hundred and twenty-one thousand, seven hundred, and thirty-nine persons. It's truly remarkable when the woman leading the prayer forgives 'those who trespass against us' after her husband's assassination.

Following the oath of office, the Chief Justice of the Supreme Court formally introduced Michelle Oobima to America and the world,

"Ladies and Gentlemen: the 47th president of these United States of America; Michelle Oobima."

There was a deafening roar for a few minutes. Two-point three million people can make a lot of noise.

"Hello, America."

"ROOOOOOOOOOAR!" the crowd boomed in a 90-second response.

"Thank you, once again, for believing in the audacity of hope."

"ROOOOOOOOOOAR!" the crowd boomed again, recognising the reference to one of her late husband's most famous speeches.

"I love your enthusiasm, but please, let me, let me get this out." The inaugural address was being shown around the National Mall on massive screens. The crowd seemed to settle as they saw an obviously emotional Michelle fighting back tears.

"You met our two little girls, Malia and Sasha in 2008–ow two amazing young women who just fill me with pride." The crowd was gonna roar again, but she held up her hand for silence.

"I wouldn't be here without them today," she continued. "They, and you: the good people of America have filled my heart with hope and faith. Hope and faith. Hope and faith in America – the generous, bighearted, optimistic country that made all of our stories possible.

"A lot has happened over these past four years. And while this nation has been tested by division and hatred and all manner of challenges – I stand before you tonight, to tell you I am more hopeful about the future of America than ever before!"

The crowd recognised a chance to get their scream on and took full advantage. It was an earth-shaking, ground quaking, window-rattling, armies battling sort of scream.

"Now I told you what my intentions were during the election. They haven't changed. We believe that health care in America is not a privilege for a few, but a right for everybody. We believe that climate change is real, and we're going to provide solutions that reduce our carbon footprint while simultaneously growing our renewable green economy.

"We will put policies in place to protect Americans from senseless gun violence." She raised her left hand which was missing two fingers up beside her face," It was difficult to imagine that so many people could be so quiet.

"This won't be easy, and this won't be quick. But I still believe in the audacity of hope!

"So today, I'm here to tell you that the task ahead of us is enormous. We have more work to do for every American who doesn't have paid leave, or paid maternity leave, or hopes for a decent retirement. More work to do for every child who needs a sturdier ladder out of poverty or a world-class education. More work to do for everyone who has lived in fear these past four years. We have more work to do to make our streets safer and our criminal justice system fairer; our homeland more secure, and our world more peaceful and sustainable for the next generation. We're not done perfecting our union, or living up to our founding creed – that all of us are created equal and free in the eyes of God."

Good speakers know when their audience needs a break. The big screens showed people in the massive crowd sobbing tears of joy.

"That work starts now. And we'll need your support. Fair to say, this was not your typical election. It was not just a choice between two parties or policies; the usual debates between left and right. This was a more fundamental choice – about who we are as a people, and whether we stay true to this great American experiment in self-government.

"Look, the Independent People's Party will always have plenty of differences with the Republican Party and the Democrats, and there's nothing wrong with that; it's precisely this contest of ideas that will push our country forward.

"But what we heard from Donald Trimp the past three and a half years wasn't particularly Republican and it sure wasn't conservative. What we heard was a deeply pessimistic vision of a country where we turn against each other, and turn away from the rest of the world. There were no serious solutions to pressing problems; just the fanning of resentment, and blame, and anger and hate.

"And that is not the America I know. The America I know is full of courage, and optimism, and ingenuity. The America I know is decent and generous. Sure, we have real anxieties – about paying the bills, protecting our kids, caring for a sick parent. We get frustrated with political gridlock, worry about racial divisions; are shocked and saddened by the madness of school shootings, or the madness of someone who tries to attack an ally with nuclear weapons."

The big-screen zoomed in on Elijah, and then a split screen that showed Elijah in Washington and Juliette in Ottawa with two beautiful twins that were seven weeks old. Elijah and Juliette were both beaming with pride while wiping away tears. The crowd went bonkers.

"Let's not try to deny what we have seen with our own eyes, and heard with our own ears. This madness, this raging hatred, and this division are still with us. Trust us, it's real." She motioned to her fatherless daughters. "So we're challenged to do better; to be better. But as I've traveled this country, through all fifty states; as I've rejoiced with you and mourned with you, what I've also seen, more than anything, is what is right with America. I see people working hard and starting businesses; people teaching kids and serving our country. I see engineers inventing things, and doctors coming up with new cures. I see a younger generation full of energy and new ideas, not constrained by what is, or what was, but ready to seize what ought to be!"

The crowd was getting into the rhythm now, cheering in shorter spurts, at each measured pause.

"Most of all, I see Americans of every party, every background, every faith who believe that we are stronger together – black, white, Latino, Asian, Native American; young and old; gay, straight, men, women, folks with disabilities, all pledging allegiance, under the same proud flag, to this big, bold country that we love.

"That's the America I know.

"My late husband..."

The new president was drowned out by a massive roar. She let them - and Barack- have their moment, then raised a hand to ask for silence.

"My late husband once told me: Michelle, nothing prepares you for the demands of the Oval Office. Until you've sat at that desk, you don't know what it's like to manage a global crisis or send young people to war. But near the end of his second term, he realised that if anyone ever understood how hard it is to be president, it's likely the president's partner. Trust me. Please. Trust us. I know what's at stake in the decisions our government makes for the working family, the senior citizen, the small business owner, the soldier, and the veteran. Even in the middle of a crisis, we will listen to people, and keep our cool, and treat everybody with respect. And no matter how daunting the odds; no matter how much people try to knock us down, we will never, ever quit on you."

The screen showed the scene of carnage on Veterans Day at Arlington when 68 people were murdered; her husband was now listed among the dead on a massive memorial at the same site where he was assassinated.

President Oobima spoke more quietly now. "See, here's the thing. I'm not gonna Make America Great Again. America was already great. We've slipped, and we may have stumbled, but we're not down, and we're not out. And I promise you, our strength, our greatness, does not depend on any single person acting as a saviour. In this recent election, you spoke loudly, and you were heard. And that, in the end, might be the biggest difference in this election – the meaning of our democracy.

"'Ronald Reagan called America *'a shining city on a hill.'* We are not fragile or frightful people. We will not cower in fear. Our power comes from those immortal declarations first put to paper right here in Philadelphia all those years ago; *'We hold these truths to be self-evident, that all men are created equal; that together, We, the People, can form a more perfect union.'*"

The crowd went crazy.

"That's who we are. That's our birthright: the capacity to shape our own destiny. That's what drove patriots to choose revolution over tyranny and our GIs to liberate a continent. That's what gave women the courage to reach for the ballot, and marchers to cross a bridge in Selma Alabama, and workers to organize and fight for better wages.

"America has never been about what one person says he'll do for us. It's always been about what can be achieved by us, together, through the hard, slow, sometimes frustrating, but ultimately enduring work of self-government.

"And that's what we'll work towards, together with our republican, democrat and independent members. We know that this is a big, diverse country and that most issues are rarely black and white. That even when you're 100 percent right, getting things done requires compromise. That democracy doesn't work if we constantly demonize each other. We know that for progress to happen, we have to listen to each other, see ourselves in each other, fight for our principles but also fight to find common ground, no matter how elusive that may seem.

"We know we can work through racial divides in this country when we realize the worry black parents feel when their son leaves the house isn't so different than what a cop's family feels when they put on a blue uniform and goes to work; that we can honor police and treat every community fairly. We know that acknowledging problems that have festered for decades isn't making race relations worse – it's creating the possibility for people of goodwill to join and make things better.

"We know that we can insist on a lawful and orderly immigration system while still seeing striving students and their toiling parents as loving families, not criminals or rapists; families that came here for the same reasons our forebears came – to work, and study, and make a better life, in a place where we can talk and worship and love as we please. We know that their dream is quintessentially American, and the American Dream is something no wall will ever contain.

"It can be frustrating, this business of democracy. Trust me, I know. When the other side refuses to compromise, progress can stall. Supporters can grow impatient and worry that you're not trying hard enough; that you've maybe sold out.

"But I promise you, when we keep at it; when we change enough minds; when we deliver enough votes, then progress does happen. Democracy works, but we gotta want it – not just during an election year, but all the days in between.

"So if you agree that there's too much inequality in our economy and too much money in our politics, we all need to be as vocal and as organized and as persistent as Barney Saunders' supporters have been."

She paused to let those supporters show their approval for the elderly senator from Vermont.

"If we want more justice in the justice system, then we've all got to work together with mayors, and sheriffs, and state's attorneys, and state legislators. And we've got to work with police and protesters until laws and practices are changed.

"If you want to fight climate change, we've got to engage not only young people on college campuses but reach out to the coal miner who's worried about taking care of his family, we've got to engage the auto pact worker and the gas and oil drillers worried about their future in the face of rapidly changing technology.

"If you want to protect our kids and our cops from gun violence, we've got to get the vast majority of Americans, including gun owners, who agree on background checks to be just as vocal and determined as the gun lobby that blocks change through every funeral we hold. That's how positive progressive change will happen.

"I know that some people hated my late husband, and by extension myself, and our daughters and our friends and allies. We're not perfect. We've all made mistakes. That's what happens when we try. That's what happens when you're the kind of citizen Teddy Roosevelt once described. Not the timid souls who criticize from the sidelines, but someone *'who is actually in the arena…who strives valiantly; who errs, but who knows, in the end, the triumph of high achievement.'*

"And if you're serious about our democracy, you can't afford to stay home just because we might not align with you on every issue. You've got to get in the arena with us because democracy isn't a spectator sport. America isn't about yes we will. It's about yes we can.

"This got me thinking about the story my husband told you twelve years ago tonight, about his Kansas grandparents and the things they taught him when he was growing up. They came from the heartland; their ancestors began settling there about 200 years ago. They were Scotch-Irish mostly, farmers, teachers, ranch hands, carpenters, builders: hardy, small-town folks. Some were Democrats, but a lot of them were Republicans. Barack's grandparents explained that they didn't like show-offs. They didn't admire braggarts or bullies. They didn't respect mean-spiritedness or folks who were always looking for shortcuts in life. Instead, they valued traits like honesty and hard work. Kindness and courtesy. Humility, responsibility, helping each other out.

"That's what they believed in. True things. Things that last. The things we try to teach our kids.

"And what his grandparents understood was that these values weren't limited to Kansas. They weren't limited to small towns. These values could travel to Hawaii; even the other side of the world, where his mother would end up working to help poor women get a better life. They knew these values weren't reserved for one race; they could be passed down to a half-Kenyan grandson, or a half-Asian granddaughter; in fact, they were the same values my parents, the descendants of slaves, taught their our family living in a humble bungalow on the South Side of Chicago."

The big-screen showed Michelle's parents, who were crying tears of joy.

"My parents, your parents, our parents, knew these values were exactly what drew immigrants here, and they believed that the children of those immigrants were just as American as their own, whether they wore a cowboy hat or a yarmulke; a baseball cap or a hijab.

"America has changed over these past few years. But these values our grandparents and parents taught us – they haven't gone anywhere. They're as strong as ever; still cherished by people of every party, every race, and every faith. They live on in each of us. What makes us American, what makes us patriots, is what's in here." Michelle put a hand over her heart, and the audience shouted their approval.

"That's what matters. That's why we can take the food and music and holidays and styles of other countries, and blend it into something uniquely our own. That's why we can attract strivers and entrepreneurs from around the globe to build new factories and create new industries here.

That's why our military can look the way it does, every shade of humanity, forged into common service. That's why anyone who threatens our values, whether fascists or communists or jihadists or homegrown demagogues, will always fail in the end.

"That's America. Those bonds of affection; that common creed. We don't fear the future; we shape it, embrace it, as one people, stronger together than we are on our own. That's what we understand, that's the America we're fighting for.

"So for all the tough lessons, the trials and tribulations we've endured; for all the places we've fallen short; for all the times we've been knocked down, I'll tell you what's picked me back up, every single time.

"It's been you. The American people.

"It's the letter I keep on my wall from a survivor in Ohio who twice almost lost everything to cancer, but urges me to keep fighting for health care reform, even when the battle seems lost. Do not quit.

"It's the painting I keep in my private office, a big-eyed, green owl, made by a seven-year-old girl who was taken from us in the Newton school shooting, given to me by her parents so I wouldn't forget – a reminder of all the parents who have turned their grief into action.

"It's the conservative in Texas who said she disagreed with me on everything but appreciated that, like her, I try to be a good mother.

"It's every American who believed we could change this country for the better, so many of you who'd never been involved in politics, who picked up phones, and hit the streets, and used the internet in amazing new ways to make change happen. You are the best organizers on the planet, and I'm so proud of all the change you've made possible.

"Time and time again, especially over these past few months, you've picked me and my family up. I hope, sometimes, we picked you up, too. Today, I ask you to do for all of us what you did for me. I ask you to carry your brothers and sisters the same way you carried me. Because you're who Barack was talking about twelve years ago when he talked about hope." Michelle cranked up the volume now. *"It's been you who've fueled my dogged faith in our future, even when the odds are great; even when the road is long. Hope in the face of difficulty; hope in the face of uncertainty; the audacity of hope!"*

The crowd had been very patient. They had cheered briefly at the end of each paragraph, but hearing these words from this woman at this time broke the dam.

Michelle finished quietly. "Thank you for your support thus far. Please be good to each other: today, tomorrow, next week, next year. May God richly bless these United States of America."

It took three hours for the crowd to disperse from the National Mall. During that time, talking heads from news channels around the world discussed the greatness and depth of President Oobima's inaugural address. Emmanuel Macaroon said it was "the most emotionally charged and powerful public address that had ever been given."

Fox News was less kind. "Take away her husband's empty quotes, and the sorrow some feel for a grieving widow, and there's little substance left. The whole speech was a big nothing burger for me," Sean Hanratty stated.

After a day or two, public demand about inaugural crowd size was getting louder. Eventually, the National Park Service reluctantly released a statement.

"Due to controversy over estimated crowd sizes, the National Park Service no longer wanted to release official estimates for how many people attend events on the National Mall. Public pressure and demand for public awareness have caused us to reconsider our position, especially when the numbers for the largest, most recent crowd are verifiable by identification numbers registered at three security checkpoints. The five largest crowds ever assembled at the National Mall are as follows:

1. President Michelle Oobima's inauguration, 21 Jan 2021: 2,321,739 (Verified.)
2. 'Resistance Rally', 23 Apr 2019: 2,100,000 (Estimated.)
3. President Barack Oobima's inauguration, 20 Jan 2009: 1,800,000 (Estimated.)

4. President Barack Oobima's inauguration, 20 Jan 2013: 1,000,000 (Estimated.)
5. 'Million Man March', 16 Oct 1995 and 16 Oct 2015: 1,000,000 (Estimated.)

"*Fake News!*" the Trimp siblings and Trimpanzees tweeted angrily.

***

CHAPTER 7:

Climate Refugees

SimpleTown

The SimpleTown Community Hall was packed. The Guinness Book of World Records had just named "The Hall' as the largest log structure on earth. It was built of locally harvested logs and planks with a design like an arena.

"There are 1300 people who live in SimpleTown," KT Burfitt was telling CBC viewers proudly, "and they're mostly all here today waiting for our new friends." KT was a former journalist who had recently been elected as a community elder by her peers.

"What should people know about SimpleTown?" the CBC reporter asked.

"Well, they should know Simpletons have big hearts," KT responded thoughtfully. "We refer to ourselves as Simpletons, because we have embraced a simpler lifestyle.

We do most things here by hand. We grow our own food in sustainable ways. We are one of the most self-sufficient communities in North America. We share everything we have, and we have zero unemployment."

The crowd in the hall began to cheer loudly.

"It seems like SimpleTown's newest citizens are arriving," the reporter said. The camera swung over to the arena entrance, where people were being greeted warmly as they stepped nervously into their new world from six school buses. "What can you tell us about their journey?"

"Well, it began with an application to our federal government under the Immigration Act," KT said. "We indicated that our community wanted to sponsor 20 families from Sudan."

"Why Sudan?"

"My daughter Susanna and I went there on a mission with the United Nations Development Program. The Sudanese people have been very hard hit by climate change. The land these folks used to traditionally farm is turning to desert. It's gotten hotter and drier, the women were walking 15 kilometres to get water, and whatever crops the men planted withered in the ground," KT explained. "So 20 of our local families applied to sponsor 20 Sudanese families. Each host or sponsor family has arranged accommodations for our new arrivals."

The crowd in the arena erupted in cheers as Elijah and Juliette entered, each carrying one of the twins in a papoose. "Were you expecting the prime minister and the minister of youth to visit?" the CBC reporter seemed pleasantly surprised.

"They called yesterday and asked if they could attend, but they also asked that we keep it quiet," KT said.

As the news cameras rolled, the 20 Sudanese families were welcomed warmly with hugs by their host Simpleton families. "Ahlan wa salaam. Welcome to SimpleTown." The host families had learned a few key phrases in Sudanese Arabic.

"God's blessings upon your household." responded the Sudanese people. Some of them already spoke English, and those who spoke English had been training the others. They normally spoke Sudanese Arabic, their countries official language. The hosts lead their guests to chairs on the arena floor, where they sat together. The newcomers were bundled up in coats, hats, scarves, boots, and mittens that had been purchased or donated from the community. The newcomers were very shy, almost frightened. They were as tall as the Canadians but very slender. Their Canadian hosts seemed like boisterous giants by comparison.

Elijah, Juliette, (with the twins Barack and Michelle), KT, and a very beautiful Sudanese woman took the stage to thunderous applause. They were seated under a massive portrait of Queen Elizabeth taken on her coronation. The portrait was flanked by the Canadian and Sudanese flags for the occasion.

"Well hello SimpleTown," KT said from behind a podium. *Whoop Whoop!* "This is my friend Aarya Bedawi who was a teacher in Sudan. Aarya hosted Susanna and I when we visited Sudan last year." *Bigger cheers, more applause for Aarya.* "We'll be your mistresses of ceremony here for the next few minutes. Aarya will translate what I'm saying into Sudanese Arabic so that our new friends can understand and follow along with us. First, we acknowledge that we are in Salish land, the traditional ancestral territory of the Salish people. Now at this time, I'll ask you to stand, if you are able, for the playing and singing of the national anthems of Sudan and Canada."

The SimpleTown Mass Choir was very good. Many of the Sudanese people wept to hear their anthem sung so beautifully. They continued crying while 1000 Simpletons belted out O Canada. "Thank you, please be seated. I'd like to introduce our prime minister ..." KT was cut off by the roar from the crowd. After a moment, Aarya explained to the Sudanese people who Elijah and Juliette were. They stood and applauded politely along with their hosts.

"Well thank you SimpleTown for this warm welcome to our new friends and our family," *Whoop Whoop Whoop, Hubba Hubba, Applause.* "I came to Canada from Somalia

21 years ago." Elijah waited while Aarya translated. "My wife's ancestors left Africa in chains in 1771 and then came to Canada in 1870 on the underground railroad. Canada is a nation of immigrants. Canada needs more Canadians.

"To the good people of SimpleTown, thank you for having open hearts and open minds. Thank you for being decent caring people." He continued speaking while moving out from behind the podium. Elijah thought better, spoke better, connected with his audience better when he could move a little. Juliette often teased him that he spoke best when he spoke like a TV preacher. She was right.

"Brothers and sisters, the world is in trouble right now." He paused to let Aarya translate after each sentence. "Our new friends here today had to leave Sudan. They didn't want to leave, they had to leave. Their homeland and way of life were ravaged by climate change. Put yourself in their shoes today. Imagine if the roles were reversed. Imagine leaving this town and starting over in a new land. Canada needs to continue welcoming people. We are a big country. We can help people. We can help each other. We have enough room. We'll build new houses, and more farms, and grow more food. Take some time to get to know our newest Canadians. I'm sure we have so much we can learn from each other. Thank you for your kindness today. Let's be nice to each other. Ahlan wa salaam. Welcome to Canada."

***

After Elijah finished speaking, KT invited all the newest Simpleton's and their host families to start lunch. Four buffet tables and serving lines had been set up in the back of the hall.

KT and her eight-year-old daughter Susanna were the host family for Aarya Bedawi and her children. Aarya had three children: Jamal was seven, Leila was six, and Zaineb was four. "And a half." he liked to add. Susanna was a great host. She took the Bedawi children under her wing and walked them through the buffet line, explaining like a tour guide along the way.

"First, get a plate, like this, then help yourself," Susanna demonstrated, putting a bit of salad on her plate. "This is cabbage salad, potato salad, bean salad, green salad, and all those fresh vegetables." The Bedawi children and all the new Sudanese guests were wide-eyed at the sight of so much food. "Here are some noodles, and roasted barley, sweet potatoes, wild rice...if you just take a little, you can save room on your plate for the really good stuff up there." Susanna pointed to a man who was carving a whole roasted goat, and a lady serving chicken stew and dumplings.

There were hot cooked vegetables, and loaves of bread, cheeses, fruits, beverages, desserts.

"This is more food than we've ever seen," Aarya whispered to KT. They sat at long tables, with all the din and chatter of a large family. After the meal, the Bedawi children were starting to nod off.

"You must be exhausted," KT said. "Let's do up your coats, and I will show you your new house." The Bedawi's and all the other Sudanese people had been on quite a journey the past four days. They had gone from their village to Khartoum by bus, most carrying only a blanket with a change of clothes and one or 2 personal items inside. It was the first time the children had left their village, and the first time they had ridden in a bus, or been to a large city. The next day they had flown from Khartoum to Halifax in one of Canada's DART planes. It was a 13-hour flight. At the airport, they were met by some of their hosts and fitted out with warm winter clothing. Then they travelled from Halifax airport to Toronto and on to Vancouver. From Vancouver, they went to SimpleTown with some of the hosts in school buses. Everything was new to them: the weather was three degrees below zero, the ground was frozen and snow-covered.

As they walked from 'The Hall' through SimpleTown, a very large black Newfoundland dog bounded up to them. The Bedawi family looked surprised to see such a beast. "Don't worry," Susanna explained. "Muffin is very gentle, and she loves people." Susanna commanded Muffin to

"Sit," and "Shake." Each child, then Aarya gently shook Muffin's giant paw. "Good Girl Muffin," Susanna said, giving her a hug around the neck.

It was dusk, and a full moon was rising over SimpleTown, bathing the scene in a golden glow. Fluffy white clouds were letting snow fall gently on the countryside. Some Canada geese were honking loudly on the pond. A big rooster stepped out of a chicken coop, gave one surprisingly long and loud "cock a doodle doo!" and hurried back inside the coop to stay warm with the hens. In a pen beside the barn, long-haired Highland cattle, three llamas and a donkey looked curiously at the new arrivals while chewing thoughtfully on some hay. It was a magical scene. To the left of the barnyard were rows of longhouses made of logs.

"Welcome home," KT said, breaking the spell. "C'mon inside, I'll show you around. We'll be living here in Rainbow House, in number six." KT pointed at the painted sign above the door, then opened the door and stepped into the house.

"Here we can hang up coats, and take off boots so that mud doesn't get in the rest of the house. See the hooks? Put your coat up here, and put the hat and mittens in the pockets like this," KT demonstrated as she spoke. "Now put your boots over here, and, put on these slippers. See, there's a pair for each of you with your initials on them, Z for Zaineb, J for Jamal, L for Leila, and A for Aarya."

The Simpletons were famous for their wool and knitting. They made thousands of slippers, blankets, sweaters, and hats each year. It was one of many income streams that SimpleTown enjoyed.

"All good? OK, bring your things, and come with me. So, this is a parlor that we will share with other families. Come with me, and I'll show you to your bedrooms." They followed KT down a hallway, and she opened a door to a bedroom and flipped on a light. "So, gentlemen, this is your room. Jamal, it might be easier if you take the top bed, and we'll have Zaineb in the lower bed, yes?"

"Miss KT: this whole room is ours?" Jamal asked. KT knew why he asked the question. The room was almost bigger than the whole house their family had shared in Sudan.

"Yes, Jamal. Now here is a closet you can share, and some warm clothes." KT kept the tour going. "Now ladies, this is your room here across the hall." There was a large double bed, a closet, a bureau, and a makeup table with an old oval mirror. "Down the hall here is the washroom," she explained. There was an old clawfoot tub, a standup shower stall, a toilet, and a sink. The Bedawi family was speechless. It was a lot for them to take in. "Susanna and I sleep right here in this room with Susanna's artwork on the door. If you need anything, just call for me, I'll hear you. Let's sleep now, and we'll learn more in the morning yes?"

The Bedawi children and Susanna were asleep the minute their heads hit the pillows. KT and Aarya chatted, drank tea, and watched the golden moon sail like a ghostly galleon through clouds over SimpleTown and the forest beyond.

***

CHAPTER 8.

Guns Don't Kill People...

Washington

"Please. Mr. Hanratty: enough with this ridiculous argument that guns don't kill people," President Oobima responded angrily to the Fox entertainment host. Lately, whenever she spoke on this topic, she held her left hand up beside her face for emphasis. The two missing fingers she had lost to bullets spoke volumes. The gesture served as a graphic reminder for those people who might have somehow forgotten that guns had killed her husband and 68 other persons in Arlington three days after the election. The IPP president had just addressed her administration's proposed Gun Control Amendment and was taking questions.

"Yes, Amy?"

"Ma'am, can you tell us more about the corruption and bribery charges being brought against the NRA?"

"No. The attorney general will speak to that issue later today. I can tell you that the NRA is not likely to try and buy independent politicians again anytime soon." Every journalist in the room had a hand raised. The gun control amendment had passed through Congress rather easily. Essentially, the amendment involved meaningful background checks on current and future gun owners, mandatory gun safety training, a reduction in the cyclic rate of fire, and amount limits on numbers of guns and amounts of ammunition that a citizen could legally own. The IPP had won 233 seats in the House of Representatives in the 2020 election. Their votes alone could have carried it through Congress, but it also received support from some moderate Democrat representatives.

The real battleground for the bill was in the Senate. None of the 26 recently elected Independent senators were on the NRA payroll. Most of the 33 Republicans still in the Senate were obvious NRA gun whores. Trimp's visibly blatant and cavalier crimes during his reign of terror had emboldened his GOP senators. They didn't even try to hide their crimes near the end of his administration.

Unfortunately for the Gun Control Amendment, 19 of the 41 Democratic senators still in office were also beholden to the National Rifle Association. 19 plus 33 equalled 52 senators likely to vote against any sort of gun control. President Oobima knew that passing any gun control legislation would always be difficult. She had watched her husband try for eight years. The IPP amendment needed 51 votes in the Senate to be passed into law.

'*Just Follow The Money*' was the headline of an editorial piece from the *NY Times*. The article drew direct lines from Russian mobsters and oligarchs who gave rubles to the National Rifle Association. The NRA team "washed it" and gave it to most of the GOP senators and some of their democratic party counterparts. Buying American politicians was not a new thing: it had been accepted practice by both parties in DC for many years.

Big pharmaceutical companies and big health care companies had kept corporate profits astronomically high by ensuring well-funded politicians voted against affordable Medicare and PharmaCare. It was easy for corrupt politicians to ignore the fact that poor people couldn't afford medicine or medical treatment when companies kept giving them millions of dollars. Likewise, the American military-industrial complex - the world's largest publicly funded business - had kept their shareholders happy by keeping politicians well lubricated.

Bridges and roads, schools, public works, and public buildings still had to be built and maintained. Those companies who paid off the most politicians were rewarded with the biggest contracts. '*Pay to play*' had become the American way. If you didn't contribute massive amounts of money to a Republican or Democratic politician's campaign, you didn't get to play. The more money you contributed increased your chances of getting that major government contract or ensuring that your insulin prices stayed high.

To the horror and dismay of major corporations, the independent politicians did not follow the *'pay to play'* rules. In the 2020 election, the Federal Electoral Commission capped donations to independent politicians at $2700.00. By contrast, a corporation could donate $834,000.00 to a Democrat or a Republican politician. During the 2020 campaigns, the independent candidates wisely used their Republican and Democratic opponents' big money against them. The independent politicians were not owned by any major corporations. The independent campaigns had been sponsored by individuals who had donated five, 20, 50, or 100 dollars to their campaigns. Grassroots individuals had defeated the big corporations.

'NRA PRESIDENT CHARGED WITH ATTEMPTED BRIBERY' was *The Washington Post* headline that afternoon. The accompanying photo showed an enraged Todd Nugent in the NRA offices being handcuffed by the FBI. Nugent had allegedly tried to bribe six high-profile independent politicians to speak out against their party's gun control amendment proposals.

Todd Nugent's arrest for attempted bribery was one of many that had occurred recently. Executives from

Monsanto and Dow Chemicals, along with a host of big banks, pharmaceutical companies, and defence contractors were all out on bail awaiting trial. The Monsanto executive was attempting to board a flight heading to Rio de Janeiro when he was re-arrested for violating his bail conditions.

Nugent's arrest was a humiliation piled on top of all the other recent humiliations the Trimpanzees had been plagued with. Their cult leader Trimp was in prison, and many more of his family members, enablers, and supporters were on trial. Rudy Ghouliani had stroked out during Trimp's trial and was on life support. A recently leaked medical report listed Ghouliani as 'brain dead for the last three months.'

"It's been a lot longer than three months..." was a common response.

Trimp's spiritual advisor Paulette White was in prison for embezzlement and inciting hate crime. Mitch MacDonald, the former Senate House Leader had lost his seat in the election. As had Senators Gym Jordan, Randy Paul, and Devin 'The Cow' Nunez. Every day that passed revealed new horrible revelations of awful crimes Trimp's administration had committed.

Crimes against the environment that could have only occurred under a castrated and handcuffed EPA.

The litany of crimes had originally been sold to the public disguised as a way to Make America Great Again.

Unfortunately, everything that Trimp's administration enacted only served to enrich the already wealthy one percent of Americans at the expense of the other 99 percent.

Oddly, and notwithstanding the mountain of undeniable factual evidence highlighting that Trimp's administration was evil, he still had a powerful legion of supporters. The identifiable Trimpanzees were blindly, fanatically loyal to Trimp. The majority of them were willfully and proudly ignorant of Trimp's sins and heavily armed.

The small minority of Trimpanzees not heavily armed were more difficult to identify. They were the people with the most to lose and were therefore the most dangerous. They owned TV stations and newspapers, social media platforms, oil companies, dirty mines, unsafe power plants, aluminum mills, manufacturing plants, and mega-farms. These people had thrived and prospered under Trimp's reign of deregulation. First, they benefited bigly from his tax cuts to the wealthy. By removing, restricting, or castrating environmental protection and public safety as a requirement of doing business, the costs of running a coal mine, meatpacking plant, smelter, asbestos quarry, or pesticide factory were lowered significantly.

So in boardrooms and shop floors across America in 2017, unscrupulous business owners quickly noticed that Trimp's administration intended to MAGA, and did what people will often do when regulations are relaxed.

"Jim, there's no federal inspectors any more. President Trimp, God bless him, is taking the brakes off this economy and letting us regulate our own industry. Now our last quarterly report tells us we spent a lot of money on filtering our effluent before it leaves the mill. Instead, let's just run that effluent straight into the river."

"Sir, won't that hurt the river? I mean, isn't that why we installed the filters and maintain the filter plant?"

"Now Jim don't get all Greta Tunberg on us. It's a big river, and we're only putting in a l'il trickle. Those Greenpeace kumbayah people from Oobima's government are all gone." At this point, the boss would usually pour Jim another slug of bourbon and /or order a couple more beers. "'*The only solution for pollution is dilution*' my Pappy used to say. We won't hurt that old river with the l'il bit our plant puts in there. We'll employ the 30 fellers from the filter plant on the shop floor and increase production by adding another shift from midnight to 8. It'll increase our profits by at least seven per cent. Now look, Jim, if you can make this work, you'll notice it reflected in a couple of places. You'll see it in a quarterly bonus of course, and you know that we're good to the folks that are good to us here at RamJack. But I also sit on the selection committee for our State University's football scholarships. That son of yours would be a great addition to Coach Tuberville's backfield."

The 'Jims' of the world found it hard to resist both a tempting bonus and a chance to see their son play for State. *Besides,* the Jims thought, *if I don't do it, they'll fire me and promote a guy who will...*

This type of warlord capitalism allowed many companies to grow rapidly, lowering costs and unemployment and increasing corporate profit significantly. So it had seemed for a few years like Trimp was indeed Making America Great Again. Anyone who said otherwise was labelled a snowflake, libtard, whiner, tree hugger, socialist...

The one-percenters knew their people. They understood that the threat of gun control amendments being enacted by a black female president pissed off their most radical employees. The one-percenters also feared the next change coming from Michelle Oobima's administration was environmental and public safety regulation that would cut into their bottom line. Todd Nugent's arrest was the latest good excuse to take some action and slow that liberal lefty snowflake tide.

What followed Nugent's arrest was a wave of violence. Barney Saunders was assassinated in Vermont by a car bomb. The blast also killed 3 staffers and injured 11 others. In Minnesota, independent Representative Ilhan Omarr was killed by a suicide bomber with terminal cancer who left a really unsettling letter explaining his motives. An hour later, independent Congresswoman Alexandria Occasional-Cortez was wounded in an attack that killed 5 and wounded 33 others.

The following day, the Gun Control Amendment was defeated on the Senate floor. The final vote was 52 against, and 48 in favor.

***

CHAPTER 9.

A New Use for Black Gold?

Ottawa

Canadian members of parliament were discussing a topic that had been a hot button issue for politicians for many years: what to do with Alberta's oil fields. They were hearing a brief from two of the University of Alberta's engineering professors. Less Izmore, the Finance Minister, gave them the floor.

"Thank you, Sir; we're honoured to be here today. My name is Lucy MacIssac, and I'm proud to say that I was born and raised in Fort McMurray. I know a lot of people who work in the oil fields. They're proud people, and they work very hard. I have nothing but respect for these oil workers and the challenges they have faced over the past few years." *Cheers and polite applause from the floor.* "Thank you for that. Let's jump right into this." As Professor MacIssac spoke, the screen behind her provided photographs, charts, and images.

"Alberta's oil reserves are the third-largest in the world. Only the UAE and Venezuela oil reserves are bigger. Alberta's oil has been a major economic driver in Canada for more than fifty years. It has been producing 2.8 million barrels of bitumen daily. The oil from tar sands has been both a blessing and, more recently, a curse. You understand how it's been a blessing. Let me explain how we have come to think of it as a curse. Currently, the oil is trading at $40.00 per barrel. That is not a very good price when viewed historically. Bitumen has long, large carbon molecules that contain asphaltene, so it needs to be upgraded or diluted to make it 'thinner' or 'fluid' enough to be transported. Therefore, oil trapped in tar sands has always been expensive to produce and difficult to refine and transport. So we have been pit mining the sand and then burning natural gas to turn water into steam, and we've been 'steaming' the oil out of the sand. It takes a tremendous amount of energy and water to produce a barrel of oil in Alberta. As the world becomes more aware of climate change, our Alberta oil has gotten a lot of bad press. People think it's dirty and dangerous. In defence of our oil industry standards in Canada, those people are wrong." (*more cheers from the floor.*)

"But those people are also right," The floor stopped buzzing and listened more closely.

"You see, no matter how rigorous we make our environmental standards, if we are mining this oil to burn it as a fuel, it's always going to be dirty and dangerous. Our oil industry regulations are the most stringent in the world, but they can't change the laws of physics and chemistry. When we burn oil and gas, it releases carbon, which speeds global warming and climate change. This explains how we have come to view Alberta oil as a curse. We need to heat our homes and buildings somehow. We need to fuel our vehicles, cars, trucks, planes, trains with something. We need to make electricity somehow. We have become reliant on all these things. Alberta oil has done all that for us. It's heated our homes, and fueled our vehicles, and given us electricity at tremendous value. People tell us it's too valuable to leave in the ground, so we think we have to refine it and burn it. I'll say that again. We think we must refine and burn oil to keep our economy and way of life from collapsing." Lucy said the last sentence quietly. She took a few steps back.

"So let's discuss other options for the tar sands. Let's use it for other things," the second professor offered optimistically. "Good morning. My name is Robert Aloo, but please just call me Bob." *Chuckles and applause from the MPs for Bob Aloo.* "It takes four metric tonnes of Alberta tar sand to make a barrel of oil. After we steam the oil out of it, and refine it, and ship it, there's no profit in this, especially at $40.00 a barrel." The screen behind Bob Aloo kept rolling with flashing images of massive trucks, earthmovers, refineries, pipelines, oil tankers ...

"We've already discussed that digging, refining, transporting, and then burning oil is dirty and dangerous. So let's not burn it. Let's use it to make carbon fibre. Remember, we said it takes four tons of tar sand to make a barrel of oil. Four tons of tar sands will yield 35 kilograms of carbon fibre valued at $7.00 per kilogram." Bob Aloo paused while the MPs whistled, hooted, and applauded. After a moment, several began reaching for calculators. Bob Aloo raised a hand.

"245 dollars is the number you're looking for." MPs throughout the room silently dropped cellphones back into pockets and briefcases. "But what can we make with this carbon fibre, is your next question, or should be." The MPs laughed and nodded assent. Bob clapped his hands, and a team of students began lugging in all sorts of things. "Carbon fibre can be used to make beams and trusses and all sorts of building material, including boards and sheeting. It can be molded to make frames and body parts for planes, trains, buses, bicycles, motorcycles, and automobiles. It is stronger than steel and weighs 40% less. We can make light poles, windmill towers, conduits, storage tanks, micro-electrodes, furniture, and protective clothing from carbon fibre. We can make industrial equipment and tools from carbon fibre: knives, wheelbarrows, mills, screws, nuts, bolts, hammers, scissors, saw blades, drill bits, grinders, frames for glasses, computers, washers, dryers, stoves, televisions, batteries and medical equipment." Professor Aloo paused to catch his breath. The floor of the House of Commons was full of students and all the products Bob had just described.

"Why don't we take a few minutes and look at all these items and talk to these students?" Less Izmore suggested. The MPs didn't hesitate: there is nothing like actually touching and feeling a thing - anything - to make it seem more real. Within a minute, they were lifting beams and car doors and riding carbon fibre bikes. Under the students' direction, 12 volunteer MPs assembled a carbon fibre shelter, 10 meters wide and 20 meters long, and 5 meters high. Nuts, bolts, trusses, studs, sheeting, doors: everything in the building was carbon fibre.

"I can't believe how light it is... this is stronger than steel?....and it won't rust?"

"So while you're all here, let us give you a cool demo," Bob suggested. "You saw 12 of your associates assemble this building in five minutes. Now, we've decided we no longer want the building here, so I'll ask Susan and Nasrim to supervise those same 12 brave volunteers..."

As the MPs watched 12 of their associates taking the building apart, Lucy narrated options. "Carbon fibre buildings offer tremendous flexibility. We could easily expand this building, or make it smaller. It's light enough to easily take apart and move to another location on a truck bed made of carbon fibre. Maybe we decide we don't want a building at all? No matter what form we mold the carbon fibre into, we can run it through a grinder and store it as a pelletized product, ready to be re-used. Uhhhh, this next part is noisy, so just step back from the grinder a bit." Susan and Nasrim ran a few 2x4 size studs through a grinder to demonstrate.

"So how do we reform the pellets back into something?" Charlie Shackleton asked.

"Great question. These products were all made on a 3D printer. The printer has a mold, and it shapes the pellets back into that mold. Show them, Susan," Lucy suggested.

Susan and Nasrim poured the pellets into a hopper on the printer. The printer buzzed and hummed and turned the pellets into bolts. Bob and Lucy conferred quietly with Less.

"Let's return to our seats to hear the rest of the brief." Less said. The MPs were buzzing excitedly amongst themselves about what they had just seen.

"OK," Lucy said. "Let's review what we just learned. Alberta tar sand can be used as fuel or to make carbon fibre.

Now let's talk about the upside of using tar sand to make carbon fibre. Tar sand as carbon fibre has six times the value of tar sand as fuel. Last year, selling tar sand as fuel generated 65 billion dollars in sales for oil companies. That's a lot of money. However, the estimated annual revenue from selling tar sand as carbon fibre would be 380 billion dollars." The screen behind the two professors provided the visual. "So one big upside of carbon fibre over fuel is money. Six times more money, to be precise." The House of Commons members whistled, hooted, applauded.

"Let's discuss other benefits of using the tar sands as carbon fibre instead of as fuel," Bob Aloo continued. "The second benefit of carbon fibre is the sustainability of our planet's resources. When we burn tar sand as a fuel, that's it. It's been consumed and contributed to more climate change. When we use it as carbon fibre, it can be re-used, re-tooled, re-shaped, re-cycled, re-purposed. When we use carbon fibre to make things, we reduce the pressure on dwindling resources like metal and concrete. Carbon fibre is more sustainable than many resources we currently use to make 'things.'"

Bob stepped back and tagged Lucy as she stepped forward. "Benefit # three. Using tar sand to make carbon fibre is far more environmentally friendly than burning it as a fuel. When we burn oil or gas, it emits carbon dioxide. Humans burning carbon-based fuels are responsible for rapid rises in the earth's temperature. 80 per cent of the greenhouse gases in bitumen happen at combustion. This effect is negated when the bitumen is used to make a value-added product instead of a fuel. The carbon isn't released to make carbon fibre: it remains locked into the product."

"Increased employment is benefit # four," Bob Aloo said. "Currently, 660,000 Canadians work in the oil and gas sector. This includes those people who work directly for oil companies in Alberta and Saskatchewan and people who deliver home heating fuel, drive fuel trucks, run gas stations, and work the refineries. That is a lot of jobs."

"Shifting those jobs from oil and gas production to carbon fibre production would create 1.4 million new jobs," Lucy said. The MPs hooted and applauded. Less Izmore whispered in her ear, and Lucy nodded. "The Minister asked for clarification on those numbers. The 1.4 million jobs in carbon fibre production would be 'new' jobs in addition to the 660,000 thousand people employed in oil and gas production currently." The MPs hooted and applauded louder this time.

Lucy gave the MPs a minute to recover. "OK. The carbon fibre jobs will look like this. The same hardworking folks that operate heavy equipment to dig up oil sands and drive it to a processing plant can keep doing just that. The people who extract oil from tar sands will be retrained to extract asphaltene instead. Asphaltene is what we use to make carbon fibre. It's a long carbon molecule that is predominant in our tar sand. It's what makes our oil heavier and more expensive to process than lighter oils. It's also precisely what gives us a competitive advantage in a world hungry for affordable reusable building materials. We've got more easily accessible asphaltene than any other country on earth. The people who work in oil refineries can be retrained to do asphaltene extraction and carbon fibre production. Job gains? We see the biggest job gains in two places: transforming our energy grid and manufacturing."

Lucy tagged Bob back in. "Transforming our energy grid will be a huge employer. We see the potential for 800,000 new jobs in this field. "Bob paused to let the MPs whistle, cheer, and clap. "Specifically, we see 300,000 jobs in the next five years in upgrading and increasing the capacity of our electrical grid. We still need and want to heat buildings and fuel vehicles somehow. Here's the tradeoff. We switch from oil-based heat to heat from electricity generated by solar, wind, hydro, and thermal sources. Instead of a gas or oil furnace in buildings, we would use heat pumps, electric furnaces, electric boilers, solar thermal, and geo-thermal systems. We switch from oil-based fuel as propulsion for vehicles to electric cars propelled by electric motors. And we switch from oil, coal, and gas-fired turbines that generate electricity to electricity generated from solar, wind, hydro, and tidal sources. To do that transformation, we need to increase our capacity to generate and deliver electricity by three hundred percent. We estimate that 300,000 people would be employed in designing, building, and maintaining an electrical grid that has three times the capacity of what we currently use. We predict another 300,000 jobs will be created in energy production to feed that electrical grid. These people will be making and installing electrical energy producers: photovoltaic panels, batteries, windmills, and hydro-electric turbines to capture power from rivers, tides, and waves."

Bob paused to catch his breath, and Lucy stepped back in. "There's going to be another 200,000 jobs created in transforming homes and buildings from oil-based heating systems to electrical-based or solar thermal heating systems. The market will need folks to make and install electric boilers, electric furnaces, heat pumps, geo-thermal pumps, and solar thermal systems in homes and buildings across the country. To summarize the transformation piece from oil to electricity: 300,000 new jobs updating and increasing grid capacity, 300,000 new jobs feeding that new grid, and 200,000 new jobs in transforming heat sources for existing buildings and homes." The MPs stood, cheering and applauding for a full minute.

Less Izmore spoke quietly to Bob and Lucy. "Dr. MacIssac and Dr. Aloo need about five more minutes to finish their brief, and then they are happy to take questions."

"Thank you, Sir. We were discussing new jobs in a carbon fibre market," Lucy said. "We predict there will be 800,000 new jobs created in manufacturing carbon fibre items. It's critically important that we do the manufacturing here to realise the full potential of this resource. Canadian history of adding value to our resources is dismal. We have been exporting raw materials like wood, steel, oil, aluminum at low prices, then repurchasing it a few months later as a finished product: a bed frame, a car, a computer, an airplane. We can keep all of those jobs in Canada and build all of those items in Canada out of carbon fibre because we have the world's biggest and most easily accessible supply of asphaltene with which to manufacture goods." The MPs were on their feet now, applauding and cheering like it was a hockey game, and Canada had just scored the game-winning goal.

Dr. Aloo spoke again. "I want to re-emphasize what Dr. MacIssac just said: it's imperative. We should not export carbon fibre as a raw material. That's not where the real money is." The MPs were listening closely again. "The real money is in manufacturing goods made of carbon fibre and then selling it. Selling it as electric cars, buses, planes, boats, bikes, trains, medical equipment, and tools. You just saw what we could make with this resource. It's cheaper to make than steel. It's lighter, and stronger, and doesn't corrode. We should not give this away for others to mold, shape, and fabricate. It's a tremendous blessing.

We need to manage it wisely." Dr. MacIssac and Dr. Aloo stepped forward together and took a bow. The MPs applauded enthusiastically. The engineering students who had displayed the various carbon fibre items stepped back into the room and bowed.

The MPs clapped louder, hooting and cheering for several minutes.

"Questions?" asked Less Izmore.

"This transformation piece all sounds very expensive," said a Conservative member. "Where are individuals going to find all this money to put in a new furnace and trade in a gas car for an electric car? On a larger scale, where will power companies find hundreds of millions of dollars needed to transform our electrical grids?"

"Great question," Lucy replied. "On an individual level, subsidies have worked well in many jurisdictions," Lucy said. "Offer people a subsidy or rebate to switch over to the new preferred technology. Recently in Nova Scotia, citizens and businesses were given up to $10,000.00 for adding solar installations to their homes or businesses. The electrical energy they produced lowered their own personal costs for the power they used. Many customers ended up pushing more power into the grid than they used, thereby earning money from the power corporation as a provider of power rather than using power and paying a bill each month. On the larger question of tripling our electrical capacity, that will require significant investment in utility companies, who will, in turn, look for financial help from municipal, provincial, and federal governments."

"And where do we - the government - find the money to pay for these subsidies and upgrades?" the member persisted.

Dr. Aloo stepped forward. "We should study and learn from what Norway did with North Sea oil. Norway owns that oil as a resource. They established a state-owned company to manage the resource. Companies that come to extract oil in Norway are heavily taxed on their profits. Those profits have resulted in a trust fund currently valued at 1.8 trillion Canadian dollars or 300,000 dollars for each Norwegian. The trust fund has been used - marginally up to four percent when needed- to ensure that Norway does not run a deficit or have any national debt. I might also mention that Norway has a top-notch cradle to the grave system of medicare and free education up to the doctorate level. Norway has achieved this extraordinary feat because it has owned and controlled the resource as a nation and taxed those corporations who wish to profit from it. Canadians should own the tar sands and the carbon fibre it produces. Not big corporations.

"Canadians. All of us."

The cheering was the loudest yet.

***

CHAPTER 10.

Schadenfreude

The White House

Hosting a State Dinner for multiple nations was always a delicate balancing act. Not all South American countries liked or trusted each other, and they all distrusted the United States. Michelle Oobima had scored a diplomatic coup in getting the countries' 13 leaders to agree to visit the US at all. Most of the invited leaders had openly mocked the invitation, telling the press that the US was far too dangerous and violent a country to consider visiting.

"Our country has a travel advisory warning our citizens not to visit the United States," Brazil's opposition leader stated. "Why would President Bolsanoiro visit the US against the advice of his own government?"

One by one, Michelle Oobima and her State Department managed to convince the various South American leaders that the meeting could have positive benefits for all of them.

The main draw for all the South Americans was a proposed trade deal with the United States and the countries that ratified the agreement. Bolivia, Peru, Paraguay, Ecuador, Uruguay, Suriname, and the Guyanas' didn't trust the larger, more muscular economies of Brazil, Colombia, Argentina, and Chile. None of them trusted Venezuela, who had badly mismanaged the world's second-largest oil fields and, until Trimp's presidency, were the poster child for banana republics.

"Venezuela, to their credit, has been making slow, steady progress in providing responsible government to Venezuelans," Colombia's popular president stated. "Americans have always boasted they are the 'world champions' of everything. Under Donald Trimp's corrupt heels, they have become the 'undisputed world heavyweight champion of banana republics.'" Ivan 'El' Duque Marques was a populist and former comedian, whose campaign slogan had been *'ni criminal ni ladron!'*

Trimp critics loved the slogan.

Question. "What are six words Donald Trimp can never say?

Answer. Neither a criminal nor a thief!"

Trimpanzees were outraged by the idea of a state visit from people who might speak a different language or criticize the greatest country on earth. Many took to social media to voice their displeasure.

@*TrimpIsMySavior*: *"How dare those 'Chicanos' say the United States is a dangerous banana republic. We should just nuke the whole buncha them, teach em all who's Boss. We are! America! Trimp 2024! MAGA! KAG!"*

The responses were just as entertaining.

@*TrimpIsMySavior*: *that's lazy racism. You are living proof that America's schools are failing.*

1. *'Chicanos' is a term used to identify Mexican Americans, often proudly, by Chicanos like me.*
2. *Mexico is not part of South America. The state visit is for South American countries.*
3. *'Nuking' an entire continent would have a hazardous effect on global health. Even yours.*
4. *Wikipedia has a list of appropriate racial slurs for each country in S. America. Please try to be a better racist in the future. The internet can help you with the necessary research.*

Seating at the State Dinner had been given careful consideration weeks in advance. It required some research and balance to ensure that known enemies weren't seated near each other. For example, Bolivia's president, Linda Caliente, was known to hate Colombia's vice president. They were both beautiful ladies who apparently each resented the other's hotness. The Guyanese' weren't as friendly with Brazil as one might assume. Chile and

Argentina had been squabbling about under-sea mineral rights. Ecuador's president had allegedly had an affair with Bolivia's president, and Colombia's vice president hated him for it.

"Wow. It's just like high school," 'The Stone' joked with the State Department coordinators explaining this to him. "Really? I mean, what's the worst that could happen? Aren't these pretty stuffy affairs?"

Olive Smithwick was the senior member of the department. Her subordinates joked (quietly) that she'd been appointed by Roosevelt, fired by Trimp, and rehired by Michelle Oobima as a nod to living history and heritage. She had the permanent look of someone who had just consumed a glass of lemon juice. Ms. Smithwick looked around the room briefly before addressing the vice president dryly. "Sir: at the first State Dinner President Kennedy hosted, the Indian prime minister buried his salad fork in the Pakistani war minister's hand."

"Well, that's not good."

"Precisely. It almost resulted in a war. Then at Linden Johnson's first State Dinner, Princess Margaret and President Johnson engaged each other in a drinking contest which turned into a drinking and limerick contest."

"Sorry. A what contest?" the VP asked.

"A limerick contest. One contestant provides the opening line; the other must finish the limerick."

"Sounds pretty harmless. Who won?"

"The Princess. Johnson, who often boasted he could never be beaten at either contest, acclaimed Margaret the winner of both. They had traded nine limericks each and consumed shots of bourbon or Belfast Boilermakers after each limerick. It was Johnson's turn to provide the opening line for the Princess. Johnson began with:

> *'There was a young lady from Dallas'*...and Margaret finished with,
> *'who used dynamite sticks as a phallus.*
> *They found her vagina,*
> *in North Carolina,*
> *and her asshole in Buckingham Palace."*

Olive's delivery of Margaret's lines was in perfectly clipped Oxfordian English. 'The Stone' guffawed. "I can see why Johnson said the Princess won," the VP said. "That's a hell of a limerick."

"Queen Elizabeth, Margaret's older sister, failed to appreciate the humor in the story," Olive said. "You see, Mr. Vice President, Princess Margaret was filling in for the Queen at the dinner. Queen Elizabeth was giving birth to her daughter Anne at the time."

"Why wouldn't the Queen be happy that her sister beat the POTUS in a drinking and limerick contest?" 'The Stone' asked.

"I believe the Queen was embarrassed that the Princess was perceived as more fun and lively than herself. Elizabeth was likely further embarrassed that some people might infer that she was *'the asshole in Buckingham Palace.'*"

"Ahhh, got it. Well, that's a great couple of stories, Olive. Thanks for sharing." The VP checked his watch. "Hey, look at the time. Listen: I gotta run. When you finish the seating list, I approve it? Is that how this works?

"Exactly, Sir. I'll have a draft on your desk by 0800 tomorrow." 'The Stone' winked his thanks at Olive, raised his trademark eyebrow, and left the room. Ms. Smithwick sighed. "All right. Back to business. We agree that Uruguay's president is good beside Chile's president's wife. Next?"

***

Leavenworth

'The Apprentice: Leavenworth' was a big hit. Networks all over the world had picked it up. Fox viewers and loyal Trimpanzees were rapturous when describing the show. Viewers could "Live Tweet" during the show. The best Tweets (most favorable to Trimp) were shown. The very best Tweet of the week (again; most favorable to Trimp) won $10,000.00. Episode Six's winner was Dolores Calhoun. @Haystackslilsister from Stone Mountain, Georgia. Remember the famous wrassler Haystacks Calhoun? Trimp

fans sure did and wondered if Dolores really was Haystack's l'il sister. Fox researchers confirmed that Dolores was the real deal.

@Haystackslilsister : Merciful Redeemer, I cry after every episode. How did we ever put such a brave, honest, and generous man in prison? @RealDonaldTrimp is just like Jesus, bravely suffering for crimes Crooked Mallory Clifton and Nervous Nancy Pillosi committed. When AMERICA'S REAL PRESIDENT and the Rev. White prayed with that prisoner in episode six, and then the prisoner was released, and now his wife can walk, and his child can see? Oh, my heart!"

Trimpanzees were unaware that most people worldwide were watching it as a feel-good comedy. You know, the kind of show you watch after a bad day at work? The kind of show that makes you realise your own life isn't so terrible. You could be this poor schmuck.

The Germans call it schadenfreude. The Oxford Dictionary describes schadenfreude as *'deriving pleasure, satisfaction, or joy in the misfortune or misery of others less fortunate.'*

Have you seen those *Funniest Home Video* shows? People watch them because it's funny to see a man get kicked in the testicles by a cow or smashed in the testicles by a four-year-old swinging a golf club. Be honest. As long as it's not our own testicles being club smashed or cow kicked, we will laugh. That's schadenfreude.

"Have you seen the new *'Apprentice'* yet?"

"No. Is it awful?

"Awfully bad! I mean, sure, it's a shitshow and a train wreck. It's this season's *'Honey Boo-Boo'* but with a stupider main character. Some of the prisoners and guards have cool stories, but seeing Donald Trimp in prison, acting all aggrieved and innocent? Priceless. You can tell even the prisoners and guards know that Trimp's a moron..."

Episodes one through six followed the same storyline. Trimp meets a prisoner or a guard who's got a great story. A kindly and fatherly Trimp makes a case that the prisoner was unjustly tried and accused and/or the guard has had some bad breaks. Trimp's generosity and/or intervention with the warden helps both men's families, the prisoner is released, and the guard is promoted with a pay raise. Trimp and his spiritual advisor Paulette White pray with the prisoner and guard for their salvation; the guard's 450-pound wife gets an extra-large electric wheelchair so that she can get to church...

But episode seven went differently right from the start. "Hi, folks. I'm Sean Hanratty. Welcome to FOX's first live version of *'The Apprentice: Leavenworth.'* Hold on to your MAGA hats!"

The show seemed normal for the first minute or two. Trimp was talking to a heavily tatted prisoner named Jesus Gutierrez about the prisoner's parole chances. Trimp was pronouncing his name as *Jee-zuz*. *Hay-Zeus* thought briefly about correcting Trimp, but...*he might stop helping me.*

Then shit got real weird, real fast.

Trimp's regular guard 'Big Bobby Clobber' suddenly shot two other guards. One in the face and one in the back.

"WTF just happened there? Did you see that?"

People watching at home sat up straighter in their chairs as a cameraman shot two more guards. Out in the exercise yard, viewers watched as three more guards in towers were shot by co-workers. For a few minutes, chaos reigned. Viewers watched as about 30 more prison staff were shot or tasered and handcuffed by other prison staff, now suddenly wearing MAGA hats.

"Camera two, close up on Trimp," the director said.

"Was that real? or just part of the show? cuz that looked really real?"

"Dad, why would some guards shoot other guards?"

"Hi, America. Don't adjust your sets," Trimp said smugly. "Remember. I told you I always win." A huge guard named Big Bobby Clobber could be seen in the background speaking into a hands-free headset and nodding. Big Bobby had been seen on the show in every episode. He was Trimp's personal guard.

"All secure, Mr. President." Big Bobby said proudly.

"Nice work Big Bobby. Real Americans won't forget what you did today." Trimp gave the big guard a knuckle bump and swung back to face camera two. "Isn't he just the greatest? Big Bobby Clobber everybody. I told you I only hire the best people. Look, most of the prison staff, including my good friend Warden Cantrell, and all you Real Americans know that I'm an innocent man. All I ever wanted to do was Make America Great Again. And I did. While I was president, America was Great Again. People are saying, maybe the greatest ever. But the Looney Left doesn't want America to be great again. That's why 'Nervous Nancy' and 'Shifty Schiff' tried to impeach me. When that didn't work 'Crazy Barney,' and 'Muslim Michelle' started an illegal political party. Then they ran a FAKE ELECTION without me, your real president." Trimp paused, looked offscreen, then gave a big smiley two thumbs up. "Well, I have three special guests with great news. C'mon in kids'!"

Eric and Don Jr. proudly strode on stage to some tremendous canned studio applause. Trimp looked through his sons, then around the stage, confused, disappointed. "Where's your sister?"

"Tiffany?" Eric asked.

Trimp slapped Eric hard across the face.

"Dad, Ivanka couldn't make it," Don Jr. said quickly. "She's in China, launching a new handbag line!"

Trimp looked heartbroken. "Take us to commercial," he whispered to Junior.

"We'll be back with that 'Great News' right after this message from our sponsor: the National Rifle Association." Don Jr. said, smiling into the camera like a 1970's hair tonic shill.

"I'm Eric," said Eric sadly, to no one in particular. His face was still red from his father's slap. You could still see the tiny handprint.

****

Washington

"Madam President, FLASH Message for you," the Duty Officer whispered quietly to Michelle and 'The Stone.' They had just sat down with 125 guests at her administration's first State Dinner. A FLASH Message rarely meant good news and would not keep until a State Dinner was concluded.

"I'll explain to our guests," the vice president said.

Michelle stood and left the dinner with the Duty Officer as inconspicuously as possible, which is to say, not inconspicuously at all. The host, seated in the middle of the head table of a State Dinner, is visible to all the guests. Everyone stopped eating, the delicate tinkle of sterling silver on bone china ceased, the string quartet stopped playing, and the comfortable hum of dinner chatter between guests ceased. The room became uncomfortably quiet.

'The Stone' rose and cleared his throat. "Ladies and Gentlemen: I'm very sorry. President Oobima has been called away briefly on an unexpected matter. She'll be back as soon as possible. Please, continue to enjoy the meal and each other's company." The vice president signalled to the leader of the string quartet, and the music began again. The guests gradually began eating and chatting again, but the room's energy seemed more subdued than before Michelle's departure.

Despite all the attendees' initial reluctance in attending, the trade talks had been promising. The State Dinner slowly found its rhythm again after President Oobima's departure. The servers quietly and efficiently cleared away the second course while the guests continued speaking quietly amongst themselves. The second course had been: *'A salad of roasted butternut squash, chicory, pumpkin, lettuces from the White House garden and sheep's cheese, drizzled with cider vinaigrette.'*

The head steward tinkled a bell to get everyone's attention. "Ladies and Gentlemen, your third course is Maine Lobster Kilawin Carpaccio with Baby Sprouts, FiddleHeads, and Kalamansi Jam. It will be served with a 1973 California Chardonnay." The guests applauded politely as a well-choreographed army of servers swept into action.

President Caliente put her hand playfully on 'The Stones' forearm. "Is it true that President Trimp served 'Hamberders' at his State Dinners?" she asked the VP.

"Hah, you're funny," 'The Stone' said. "He probably wanted to. But I think his wife, the First Lady, did the menus to save us from further embarrassment." *Damn, she IS hot,* he thought. "Sadly, the classiest person in the Trimp administration was a softcore porn model who married Trimp for money," 'The Stone' added in a self-deprecating tone. "But we're trying to 'Be Better' now that Trimp is a painful memory. Tell me, what would we be having at a formal dinner in Bolivia?"

"Hmmm, our cuisine is very different. This lobster is delicious, by the way, and this Chardonnay is sinful." She drained her glass, and a steward instantly replenished it. "So. Bolivian food? We eat a lot of rice and beans, but a dish you may not be familiar with is Alpaca."

"Sorry. Al what?"

"Alpaca. It's like a smaller, more delicate cousin of a llama. It's very tender and tastes like the love child of a chicken and a lamb. Or what pig wings would taste like if pigs could fly. You must come to Bolivia and try it," she teased, eyes fluttering.

"Well, llama tell you, al pack a my bags," 'The Stone' responded with a grin.

"Haha, now who is the funny one?" Linda Caliente said.

***

The Situation Room

President Michelle Oobima was in the situation room with the Chiefs of Staff and senior personnel from Homeland Security, the FBI, and the CIA. The news was terrible and unbelievable all at once. "OK- so what's our latest Intel giving us?' she asked.

"Ma'am - rogue forces loyal to Trimp have taken over Leavenworth. Those forces included the warden and 70 percent of the facility staff. They killed approximately 30 guards and have imprisoned others who won't swear loyalty to Trimp. Fox has been broadcasting the whole thing live. Hanratty has declared Trimp the rightful POTUS, and Trimp is scheduled to address the world in three minutes."

"He's still in Leavenworth, yes? Can't we just shut down the Fox transmission?"

The admiral briefing the president looked embarrassed. "Yes, he's still in Leavenworth." He paused. "And, no: we can't shut down or jam their transmission satellites. In 2019, Trimp's 'Space Force' put up a couple of their own satellites that were 'Top Secret.' They aren't connected to anything we can access through our normal systems. Ma'am: unfortunately, the satellites are dedicated to carrying FOX." President Oobima did not look happy.

The admiral was thinking of a line he learned in Annapolis as an officer cadet. *When briefing a Commander, they need all the info and facts to make the best decisions. Don't hide the bad news, and only present the good news. That just leads to bad decisions. Be brutally honest when briefing your Commanders. Always.* The admiral took a deep breath and forged ahead. "It gets worse. The satellites are tied into GPS systems worldwide. If we jam the signal or shoot it down, planes, trains, and ships everywhere will crash."

Michelle shook her head in disbelief. The admiral continued. "There's more. The Space Force satellite may have a weapon that Trimp can control. Madam President, it may take some time to jam the Fox signal and to disable or disarm the satellite. In the meantime, I think we should just watch the broadcast, for a few minutes at least, to see where this is headed."

'I'd rather gouge my own eyes out,' her inside voice said.

"Agreed," her outside voice said.

"Welcome back, viewers," Hanratty gushed to a large television audience that now included a very reluctant President Oobima. "We promised you an exciting show, and President Trimp always keeps his promises. Mr. President, I believe you have some big news for America?

"I sure do, Sean. Today, as the Real President of the Real United States, I am demanding the resignation of Fake President Michelle Oobima and all her socialist friends. The 2020 election was Fake News! Also, people are saying I was subject to really bad, maybe the worst ever, Presidential Harassment! But today, I'm back. I mean, I was never really gone. And together, with your support, we'll keep Making America Great. Again. My most loyal supporters, the Real Americans, are still with me, and it's gonna be terrific, nothing but the best, trust me." Don Jr. and Eric had never looked prouder of their Dad. Sean Hanratty was beaming.

"Now all of you know, I'm a patient man, generous and kind. I've always turned the other cheek. But the socialists and snowflakes and Do Nothing Dems betrayed me, and betrayed you, the real patriots, as well." As Trimp spoke, the cafeteria's main stage began to fill with well-known loyal Trimp supporters.

Sarah HuckleBerry-Slanders.

Todd Nugent.

Trimp's 'spiritual advisor,' Reverend Paulette White.

Shawn Spice.

Tucker Corson.

Mikki Haley.

The living Koch brother.

Tommi Lauren.

Paul Manafart.

Todd Cruz.

Reverend Frankland Graham.

The former Attorney General and Fred Flinstone stunt double Bill Bartlett.

Devin 'The Cow' Nunez.

The stage kept filling with famous Trimpists. Secretaries of Departments. State Governors.

The guy who played Chachi.

Four Supreme Court Judges.

Rudy Ghouliani, comatose, strapped in a wheelchair.

All the Fox and Friends team.

The creepy SEAL Chief Petty Officer who murdered a wounded civilian teenager with his knife and posed with the mutilated corpse.

Rodger Stone (who took his shirt off and flexed his Nixon tattoo.)

They kept coming. It was a veritable hit parade of the most devious, cruel, well known Trimpanzee's. Trimp's smug smile grew smugger and smugger.

The cameras panned out over the cafeteria floor. Hundreds of prisoners and guards wearing MAGA hats. They were all armed.

The camera's closed back in on Trimp. He looked crazier than normal. Madder than normal. Oranger than normal - like he was about to stroke out. His eyes were wild, glassy, unfocused.

"So. Michelle. I know you're watching. Let's be honest; I know everybody's watching. Real Americans love me. And

Fake Americans, the coastal elites, sipping their lattechino's, well, they love to hate me. But they're watching. Cause secretly; they love me."

Trimp paused to pretty up his hair, turning from left to right, and the audience cheered and applauded wildly. For a minute, he forgot where he was or what he'd been talking about. Jr. nudged him and whispered in his ear. "Thanks, Jr. Isn't he the greatest? He keeps me focused. *'Daddy- focus on the teleprompter,'* he just told me."

The audience dutifully cheered for Jr. "2032, 2032," they chanted. Trimp raised his hands to quiet them and willed himself back on script. Furious again.

"Michelle. You are NOT the real president. Your husband - who wasn't born in America, by the way - was also never the president. 'Nervous Nancy' Pillosi was ALSO. NEVER. THE. PRESIDENT," he screamed. "I'm gonna show you that I mean business. And then you're gonna resign. Michelle: remember when you and Crooked Mallory and Nervous Nancy and Shifty Schiff and all the liberal snowflakes put my friends and me in prison and called us deplorables? And all the relentless mocking?" Trimp's voice grew softer. Still clearly as crazy as a loon on bath salts, but with a softer voice. "Well, that hurt. And I don't like people who hurt me." Trimp turned to face his offspring. "Boys, what did I tell you to do when someone hurts you?"

"Hurt them back 10 times harder!" Jr. and Eric shouted enthusiastically.

"I tried to be nice," an enraged Trimp screamed, spittle flying. "But you Lefty Losers wouldn't let me Make America Great Again. I told you. I. Always. Win!"

Viewers at home were suddenly looking at a beautiful tropical island. Some drone footage showed sandy white beaches, palm trees, and a significant mountain range. Sean Hanratty's voice narrated the pastoral scene. "This is Bikini Atoll, in the Pacific Ocean. The island is 46 square miles, which coincidentally, is the same size as San Francisco. In 1943, the United States Air Force used Bikini Atoll to test air burst atomic weapons. Although the island looks beautiful, it still has significant radioactivity. No one lives on Bikini Atoll."

Eric and Don Jr. wheeled in a table with knobs and buttons. It looked ominous because it had a big red button, marked "LAUNCH" in bold red letters. The camera zoomed in on Junior. "Dad, you are always gonna be my Real President. I'm so proud of you right now. Now show Americans your awesome firepower."

"Thanks, Jr. This is a great moment for 'Real Americans.' When I'm reinstated as the rightful POTUS, we can use this weapon to Make America Great. Again. It's the greatest, I mean, just the best 'Space Weapon' ever. Trust me, I know more about 'Space Weapons' than all the ... 'Space Weapon' doctors and science people. Here, watch this: remember that island?"

Trimp grinned maniacally as he leaned a tiny hand backed up with some considerable bulk on the red 'LAUNCH' button. Then the camera's cut to Bikini Atoll.

The world watched in horror as a massive explosion or earthquake smashed Bikini Atoll. The island shook violently, and all the trees and plants caught fire for about 60 seconds. Then a massive wave swept in and put the fires out. The wave was high enough that the water went to the peak of the mountains. The mountain ranges collapsed, and the island started to break up. When the wave receded, there was nothing left standing. The island had been flattened and looked like melted black glass. About 30 seconds later, the island sank, leaving a huge circle of expanding ripples.

"Whoooooooohoooo!" The Trimp brothers screamed and high-fived each other. The audience was going wild. Trimp made the 'smug smile magnanimous gesture' with both arms out that he used for spectacular events. The audience went wilder. It took a couple of minutes to calm them down so that Trimp could speak again.

The camera swung back to a smiling Trimp.

"Michelle. Resign. And then declare that I'm the Real President. I'll give you 47 hours, or I'll destroy a city, right here, live on Fox. San Francisco, maybe? That's a shithole, filled with Mexicans, thieves, and rapists. And 'Nervous

Nancy' and 'Shifty Schiff' live there. Or maybe Baltimore? Or even Washington? That would 'DRAIN THE SWAMP' for sure," he shouted, pumping his fist. The prison studio audience was delirious with the Washington idea.

"Drain the Swamp! Drain the Swamp! Drain the Swamp!" they chanted.

Hanratty eventually calmed the audience down. He knew they needed to cut to commercial. Hanratty spoke quietly to Trimp, who nodded his head and reluctantly returned to the script. "What a great audience. Just the best. Stay tuned to FOX to see what happens next. One final point. A lot of stupid people will think that your FAKE PRESIDENT' 'Muslim Michelle' should nuke Leavenworth, and I'll be dead.

"But that's a bad idea. Killing me won't kill me," Trimp said. "I'll gladly give my life to MAGA, just like Jesus did. People are saying, Sean - you told me this- there are hundreds of billions of Real Americans who still want to MAGA. And the bravest and best among them have the same button I just used to destroy that island. And if I'm killed, my good friends will kill you back TEN!TIMES! HARDER!" Trimp looked like an orange demon. He was flushed and sweaty but still sporting that smug smile a vicious bully wears when kicking a smaller unconscious child.

Trimp's live TV audience applauded wildly.

"Michelle? Missus Fake President?

Remember. Here's the deal. 47 hours. You resign. I become POTUS. Again. And then we'll MAGA. Again. Or else...BOOM!" he shouted the last line as he pointed at the launch button. Trimp took a final bow. Well, he did that arms out, magnanimous gesture. He was physically incapable of bowing. He'd tip over and fall on his head. His closest and most loyal friends wrapped him in a group hug.

"That's all the time we have for tonight's show, folks," Hanratty said. Tune in tomorrow night: same FOX time, same FOX channels, for a new show we are launching. It's called: *'Trimp Resurrected: God's President!'* The new show's title was featured below a young, muscular shirtless Trimp, beaming with holy radiance. The body looked suspiciously like Rocky's. (Rocky's body from *'Rocky One,'* not *'Rocky Nine.'*)

****

The White House

President Oobima's guests were halfway through their main course when Bikini Atoll was wiped off the map. It started with one aide whispering in one president's ear. Within 60 seconds, 125 guests were watching 125 cellphones in shock and horror. Michelle Oobima returned to a room filled with panicked world leaders. Everyone was shouting and screaming. Most of the guests were headed for the exits, screaming for safe passage to the airport, where their various diplomatic planes were on standby.

"I'm truly sorry," she said. "This is horribly awkward and embarrassing. I'm sorry that this madman has resurfaced. Sadly, it appears that he has some sort of weapon. We are doing everything in our power to neutralize this threat. You are guests of the United States. We'll do everything in our power to keep you safe."

Michelle looked around the room, willing herself to remain calm for her guests. "I understand that you want to leave. If you do want to leave on your own diplomatic flights, we'll protect you to Andrew's Air Force Base immediately and provide fighter jet flight coverage to the edge of our national airspace." The room was buzzing.

"Madam President," Brazil's President Bolsanoiro said, "I believe that this madman Trimp, hates you, and hates Washington so much that this city will be the next to be destroyed. I request your military accompany and protect my delegation back to Andrew's Air Force Base. I further request the air protection you offered. I trust you and believe that your intentions are good. But America is not safe. Your country is filled with armed lunatics loyal to a madman. And now this monstrous madman has a weapon capable of great destruction. I will pray for the safety of your country. But we should never have come here. And now we should leave as quickly as possible." The other presidents and guests were nodding their heads in agreement with Bolsanoiro.

"Colonel Smith will organise convoys to the airport. Those wishing to depart Washington, see him at the rear of the room," President Oobima said. Colonel Smith raised his hand and was quickly surrounded by a large group.

"I need to be in our Situation Room. I'll leave you in Vice President John-Stone's capable hands should you have any questions. Again, my apologies." President Oobima departed surrounded by her security detail.

Colonel Smith organised the 'Leave' group very quickly. Washington's streets were already snarled with traffic from citizens fleeing the city. Five Sea King helicopters whisked the guests efficiently from the White House lawn to Andrews Air Force Base.

The guests were all gone within ten minutes. An army of servers was efficiently clearing away plates and glasses as Dwain John-Stone made his way to the situation room in the bunker beneath the White House.

***

CHAPTER 11.

A Deal With The Devil

Washington

News that a disgraced, deranged, and imprisoned former president just destroyed a Pacific island with a deadly 'Space Weapon' got around pretty quickly. An hour after Bikini Atoll was destroyed, messages and emails offering help started pouring into Washington.

Pakistan, India, North Korea, China, and Russia sent messages indicating that they were prepared to attack Leavenworth with nuclear weapons in retaliation for Trimp's latest war crime.

"We have dreamed of an opportunity to test our latest missile's long-range ability," North Korea's offer read. *"We*

look forward to annihilating your maniacal dictator for the good of the world. Respectfully:

The Supreme Leader of the Peoples Democratic Republic of North Korea,

Kong Jong Un.

13 Japanese Kamikaze pilots from WW2 offered a more moderate solution. They still flew vintage Mitsubishi planes and were collectively known as 'The Honourable Flying Angels of Death.' Their average age was 93, and their number of pilots were diminishing each year.

"Dear Madam President: please accept our feelings of sorrow and anger regarding Mr. Trimp's recent savage behavior. We are willing to fly our Mitsubishi Kamikaze planes loaded with bombs into Leavenworth. Our Squadron was trained for this purpose, to die gloriously in service to our country. Sadly, the war ended before we were able to make the ultimate sacrifice in service to our country. We would proudly help our friends in America rid the world of this menace.

We are yours to command:

The Honourable Flying Angels of Death.

"Madam President, we recommend a communiqué be sent worldwide to stop anyone from retaliating against

Trimp," her military advisors suggested. "It's possible they might kill Trimp, but also possible that forces friendly to Trimp would retaliate. This is how world wars start."

"Agreed. Do you have a draft?"

President Oobima scanned the draft the admiral handed her. "Send it."

***

Leavenworth

Trimp and his followers moved quickly after the destruction of Bikini Atoll. It could all be seen on Fox News, of course, which devoted 24 / 7 coverage to all things Trimp.

"Fear not ye worshippers of Jehovah," Reverend Paulette White told the Trimpanzees in Leavenworth. "God Almighty has chosen us to do his work on earth, and that same all-powerful God protects us. God and Donald Trimp will smite our enemies in their mercy and lead us to MAGA ... She said that much in English, then started twitching, shaking, and saying other stuff that no one could understand.

It sounded like when the Orcs talked in the *Lord of the Rings* movies.

"Yeahhhhh, I'm calling bullshit on the whole 'speaking in tongues thing,'" said most people.

"This is the Lord himself who has possessed the reverend's body, and is speaking to true believers directly through her," offered Frankland Graham. "The Lord is speaking through Reverend White in an ancient Hebrew dialect that only those whom the Lord has chosen can understand."

"Can you translate what the Lord is saying for our viewers?" Tommi Lauren asked Reverend Graham.

"Yes, of course. The Lord has blessed me with the same gift. The Lord is saying, 'Fear not ye worshippers of Jehovah. God Almighty has chosen us to do his work on earth, and that same powerful God protects us. God and Donald Trimp will smite our enemies in their mercy and lead us to MAGA.'"

"Yeahhhhh, I'm still calling bullshit on the whole 'speaking in tongues thing,'" said most people.

***

Mar a Lago

Assured of God's protection, and with the additional security offered by a 'Space Weapon,' Trimp then flew in his private jet to 'The Southern White House' from Leavenworth.

The prisoners and guards loyal to Trimp remained in Leavenworth to *secure the heartland.* Within 12 hours, nearly 50,000 loyal MAGAts had joined forces with them in Kansas.

In that same time period, Florida state troopers estimated nearly a million loyal Trimpanzees were rallying to their Messiah in Mar a Largo. All - save the richest - proudly wore the uniform: at minimum, the MAGA or KAG red hat. The better-equipped MAGAts had the whole ensemble: Trimp Army T-shirts and jackets, bumper stickers, and posters. Most arrived in trucks, with Trimp flags and significant firepower. Some came in large motorhomes. A few more rolled up in their own vintage tanks or armoured personnel carriers. A smaller percentage flew in their own cropdusters or small jets and landed on Mar a Lagos runway. 'Bikers for Trimp' rolled in by the thousands. Still more MAGAts motored in their own boats and tied up at the Mar a Lago marina.

MSNBC in Florida tried to cover the story, but the mob lit the van on fire before the news crew could get their equipment out of the vehicle.

"We've had enough FAKE NEWS," a psychotic bleached blonde lady in her 60's screamed into a FOX camera. "Y'all just keep watching FOX, and you'll learn the truth." She was wearing a star-spangled jumpsuit.

Trimpanzees, guided by Fox, were gathering together in solidarity across America. 8,000 were gathering at a ranch in Wyoming. Similar well-armed groups joined forces in Idaho, Alaska, Utah, Alabama, Oklahoma, the Dakotas, Nebraska, Georgia, Mississippi, West Virginia, and Kentucky...

The numbers were bigger in the more populated states and cities. Dallas, Phoenix, and Houston each had more than 60,000 Trimpanzees clustered together.

24 hours after Trimp destroyed Bikini Atoll, Fox News reported that 2.7 million heavily armed loyal Trimp supporters were assembled in red states across America.

***

Ottawa

Elijah often convened short notice meetings of his government's cabinet ministers. He also had senior personnel from the Canadian Forces, Canada Border Services, CSIS, and the RCMP at this particular meeting. People were still in shock that Trimp had murdered 30 prison staff, freed (and armed) the prisoners, and destroyed a remote island with a satellite-based weapon.

Elijah began. "Admiral, what's our current situation?"

At 43, Admiral Jon Poon was the youngest Chief of Defence Staff ever to hold the post. "Sir, for now at least, Trimp seems committed to his plan," the CDS said. "His short term goal is to regain the presidency through the threat of further destruction. Trimp warned the world that if he is neutralised or killed, forces loyal to him will take revenge with the satellite-based weapon he recently demonstrated. In addition to this space weapon, Trimp still has many supporters, most of whom are heavily armed. Identifiable forces loyal to Trimp include the regular suspects that have been harassing Americans since 2017: the KKK, Trimp's Army, Biker's for Trimp, Team America, the Oath Breakers, Trimp's Christian Soldiers, the 3%er's and numerous other similar civilian militia groups. These groups all have a nationalist agenda. Recent intel suggests that those supporters willing to start and fight in a civil war to put Trimp back in power range between four to seven million persons."

"That is a whole lotta crazy," Charley Shackleton said sadly.

The admiral paused briefly to look around the room. "There is a more disturbing concern than the identifiable or known groups I just mentioned. Homeland Security, the FBI, CIA, CSIS, and the RCMP know who the known groups are. The unknown Trimp loyalists could pose a greater threat." Several hands immediately went up in the room.

"I thought that might raise some questions. I'll explain what I mean by unknown groups," Admiral Poon said. "There is intel that suggests a small percentage of the American military, various police forces, and security agencies may be loyal to Trimp rather than to the duly elected government of the day. Obviously, the personnel in federal, state, or municipal security positions have sworn their loyalty to the Constitution of the United States: they can't publicly express their loyalty to Trimp over their sacred oath; they would be relieved of their duties, possibly even charged for treason. These 'unknown' Trimp loyalists pose a great danger to America simply because they are unknown and could work against the current elected administration from within their respective institutions. Understood?"

The ministers, security, and military personnel in the room nodded. Admiral Poon resumed his brief. "President Oobima has sent a message worldwide that no one should try to attack or neutralise Trimp. Trimp has relocated from Leavenworth to Mar A Lago, or, in his words, 'The Southern White House.' Our troops are all on high alert, and our Disaster Assistance Response Teams are on standby should we need to deploy them. We believe America is on the brink of civil war." The young admiral concluded his brief in the textbook manner all Canadian Forces personnel use. "Mr. Prime Minister: that concludes my brief. Do you have any questions?"

"I do," Elijah said. "Do we know the nature of the weapon used? Is there anything we can do to help reduce the threat of another attack?"

"Our best people are working on that, Sir," Admiral Poon said. The weapon itself is not nuclear in nature; there's no radioactive cloud over Bikini Atoll. It may be a laser or sonic waves designed to trigger earthquakes, but that is still speculation. The information on these systems was well protected by Space Force personnel, even from their American defense department counterparts. The satellites Trimp used yesterday were built with taxpayer's money from the defence budget. It was pushed through congress as a communication satellite for the 'Space Force.' Instead, it seems that private contractors installed Fox and Facebook's signal and platform and then installed a weapons system. As soon as we know more, we'll brief you."

"OK. Thank you, admiral," Elijah said. The Chief of Defence Staff took a seat at the oval table. "Floor's open. Ideas?" The young prime minister looked around the room hopefully.

"I've got an idea," Danni Grey Eyes said quietly. "But it's crazy."

"I think 'crazy' is likely the only kind of idea that might help us right now," Elijah said. "Spill."

"So we're gonna need buy-in from President Oobima, the Chinese, and the Russians," Danni began. "Then we'll need the United Nations for the long term plan. First: we are still holding the CEO of Huawei here in Canada, yes?"

***

Washington

"We interrupt our regularly scheduled programming with a message from the president of the United States." said almost every television set in the world. It was noon in Washington. Billions of people had witnessed Trimp's destruction of Bikini Atoll.

"I wish I could say good day," President Oobima began. "But it is not. We are going to begin this transmission with a moment of silence for the lives of 30 brave prison guards we recently lost in Leavenworth."

I'll get right to the point," the president said after a minute had passed. Michelle Oobima looked composed and sounded calm for a person in her current stressful situation. "As you are aware, a convicted criminal recently murdered 30 guards in Leavenworth in cold blood. He freed his fellow inmates and gave weapons to those inmates who swore loyalty to Team Trimp. He then blew up Bikini Atoll, a remote island in the South Pacific. Donald Trimp has demanded that I resign as president immediately and proclaim him as our new president. Trimp stated that if I do not give him what he wants, he will use that weapon to attack American cities. Now think about that. Please. Let those facts sink in for a moment." President Oobima requested viewers.

"A convicted criminal who just murdered 30 prison guards is demanding that I make him the president of the

United States," she continued. "If I do not, he says he'll kill more Americans with a weapon that his supporters built - illegally, using taxpayers' dollars - and then hid from Americans. Make no mistake. This is not a weapon controlled by American military personnel. This weapon is controlled only by Trimp supporters who are threatening to use it against other Americans." Michelle looked sad but also determined.

"I'd like to address the Trimp supporters for a moment," the president continued. "Apparently, somehow, there are still some of you who love, admire, and respect this man. Some of you murdered my husband, Barney Saunders, Dustin Trudel, 35 Guatemalan refugees, and 30 innocent corrections officers. You continue to spread hate and division and racism and nationalism around the world.

"Rational people worldwide have tried to use facts and logic and reason over the past five years to illustrate how Donald Trimp is evil and criminal and corrupt. But you have not listened. Now, the man you worship and admire is demanding to be made president again." The camera's zoomed back in on a defiant Michelle Oobima. "But that is not possible. That is not how democracy functions. Donald: NO. I will not resign. I will not acclaim that you are the lawful president of these United States.

"Instead, I have a message for you. Let's call it 'A New Deal.' Donald: you have always wanted the world to believe that you are a master negotiator. We know there are only a few things you care for and desperately need: your daughter and the undying adoration and attention of those who worship you. We are in a position to destroy what you care for. If you make the right decision, you will get to keep what you care for. Our demand is fairly simple. Have your personnel disarm the satellite weapons currently in your control and give access and control of your weaponized satellites over to NORAD personnel.

"If you do not meet our demands within twelve hours, we will be forced to take the following steps. First, your daughter will die," the president said. "Ivanka, say hello to your father. I'm sure he's watching."

Via the magic of satellite television, viewers saw that Ivanka Trimp was shackled in a tiny, filthy cell with some emaciated Chinese prisoners. She looked like she had been roughed up a little. Or a lot. Her hair had been cut by someone using garden shears or the lid from a tin can. "Hi, Daddy. Please don't blow anybody up, or..." A Chinese guard viciously kicked Ivanka in the stomach and rolled a door across the screen, cutting viewers off. The screen switched back to President Oobima in Washington.

"Second Step: we release the infamous tapes that Vladimir Poutine made in Moscow all those years ago," Michelle looked disgusted. "Donald, I saw the tapes. The Russian president just sent them to us. I vomited, and I still feel sick and dirty. I will likely never get those images of you in black rubber out of my mind. I understand why you wouldn't want the world to see this. It would absolutely shatter and destroy your already tarnished image and legacy. Even the most willfully stupid, vicious, and morally bankrupt of your friends will denounce you after seeing these images.

"Third step: we release your last 30 years of tax returns. I thought you told us you were rich?" Michelle laughed.

"Fourth step: We release your high school and college transcripts. You also told us you were smart?" The president laughed harder.

"Donald: we've literally got warehouses filled with facts that will irreparably destroy your legacy, but that's enough for the time being. Now: if you make the right decision, you'll get your daughter back, alive, of course. If you make the right decision, we won't release the tapes or your tax returns, or your transcripts. But all that discussion comes after your satellite weapons are disarmed."

Michelle Oobima looked defiantly into the camera. Her voice dripped with loathing and anger.

"Twelve hours Donald. You've got twelve hours to give us control of those satellites. Or your beloved daughter dies in a Chinese prison, and everyone in the world learns the awful truth about you. Twelve hours Donald.

"Tick Tock."

***

156

CHAPTER 12.

Killing Him Won't Kill Him?

Washington

President Oobima's phone rang in the oval hours 13 minutes after her televised address. Her communications team advised her that Donald Trimp was on line one. The two parties spoke for seven minutes. When they concluded the call, President Oobima convened an emergency meeting with her communications team in the situation room. That meeting lasted nine minutes. The White House then did a press release advising the world that President Oobima and Donald Trimp had reached a truce and that no major cities would be destroyed with a 'Space Weapon.' The White House communiqué requested that citizens remain calm and that there was no need to flee from the cities that Donald Trimp had indicated previously as potential targets. "President Oobima will address the nation shortly to clarify these points." concluded the White House Communique.

In the first minutes of the address, she explained that Donald Trimp had agreed to her terms and that the United States Air Force had taken control of the 'Space Weapon.' The world - minus the Trimpanzees - breathed a sigh of relief.

"If you are on the move right now, trying to flee your homes in San Francisco, Baltimore, or Washington: please: Stop. Listen. Your city is safe. Please return to your homes in an orderly fashion."

President Oobima continued. "I repeat. Our own American military personnel just locked the satellite weapons firing system. As collateral, at this time, we will not be releasing Trimp's Moscow tapes, his tax returns, or his educational transcripts. As further collateral Chinese authorities will continue to hold Ivanka Trimp." President Oobima paused while the camera's switched angles. She looked grim and tired. The weight and pressure of these past few months were starting to take their toll on her.

"Donald Trimp drives a hard bargain," the president said quietly. "Today, I had to do something that I never wanted to do. I did it because I feared that Donald Trimp or any of his unwell supporters might use that weapon against innocent Americans if I did not. Today, as part of the agreement to keep our country safe, I will be pardoning Donald Trimp.

"Please believe me when I tell you that this was not an easy thing for me to consider. I did this to keep our country safe from a weapon of mass destruction. I normally would never consider pardoning a monster who has given rise to such a level of hatred and racism."

The rest of Michelle Oobima's address spoke of peace and forgiveness. She said that the military would remain on high alert and the possibility that martial law may once again need to be implemented. She encouraged all Americans to return to their homes and resume their normal lives.

In the media scrum that followed her conference, President Oobima faced a lot of tough questions.

NY Times: "Why would you pardon Donald Trimp after all he's done, after all the crimes he has committed?"

President Oobima sighed. "Honestly, I'm the last person who wanted to pardon Donald Trimp. I blame Trimp for inciting the hatred that killed my husband and thousands of other innocent people. But I felt I had no choice. I agreed to pardon him to keep our citizens safe from a weapon of mass destruction."

Washington Post: "Madam President: if you pardon Trimp, do you believe he will attempt a coup?"

"Well, it's not 'if' I pardon him," the president responded. "I have pardoned him, in exchange for our security. Donald Trimp can no longer kill millions of our citizens with a...I can't believe I'm saying this in a press conference...'Space Weapon'. In exchange for that security, he insisted on a presidential pardon. Donald Trimp and I discussed why he should not attempt a coup. The Chinese government has agreed to hold Ivanka Trimp on our behalf. Should Trimp and his loyalists attempt a coup on our lawfully elected government, the Chinese will execute his daughter. We also still hold many items Mr. Trimp does not want the public to see. Trimp is aware that if he tries to lead a coup against the elected government of the American people, that his daughter may die, and all the embarrassing collateral regarding his past will be published."

MSNBC: "Ma'am, are you concerned about the number of Trimp loyalists massing in some regions? Many are heavily armed. Are you considering that we may need to impose martial law again? What steps will your administration be willing to take to Americans from attacking other Americans?"

"Great question. One minute. Let me ask our Joint Chiefs a question first." President Oobima stepped back from the podium and huddled briefly with her Joint Chiefs of Staff. A moment later, she returned to the microphone. "Sorry. I didn't want to answer your question without asking the experts. You see, I like to listen to people with expertise. The Joint Chiefs obviously know more about our military than I do." The journalists in the room laughed.

It was a pretty good burn on Trimp, who was famous for letting the public know that he didn't need experts. He knew more about ISIS than all the generals. He knew more about pandemics than immunologists. He knew more about nuclear weapons than nuclear engineers. And so on.

"Now: back to your question. Yes: of course, we are very concerned about the number of heavily armed people loyal to Mr. Trimp assembling in some regions. You asked what steps our government will take to protect Americans? Our military personnel are all on high alert: all leave has been cancelled."

Michelle continued. "I needed to ask our Joint Chiefs if our military personnel would be able to sustain another period of martial law if necessary. They assured me that they could. I also asked them to confirm how many days our country has been under martial law in the past 18 months. The answer is 93 days." She looked sad but also very determined.

"93 days. How embarrassing is that? That's an incredible amount of time for a country to exist under martial law. It's not normal for a functioning democracy to implement martial law so frequently. It's not normal that it last for such long periods of time. President Pillosi declared martial law in January 2020, after Trimp tried to attack Canada with nuclear weapons. Remember the Great Canadian Blackout?"

"That period of martial law was to prevent looting among our own populace and to stop Americans from killing other Americans over their political views. I think we can all agree that in this case, martial law was justified?" Heads all over the room were nodding in agreement. "Who remembers how long it lasted?" the president asked.

Hands were up all over the room. She pointed at Sean Hanratty, even though his arm wasn't raised. "Sean, do you recall how long that period of martial law lasted?"

Hanratty looked embarrassed. "Sean. C'mon. You did a big story on it. 21 Jan 2020. You and your network were livid that an interim president had dared to declare martial law," the president said. "You really can't recall how long it lasted?" A junior Fox reporter whispered in Hanratty's ear.

"Forty-eight days? "Hanratty said tentatively. The room groaned. Many booed. There was some hearty laughter mixed in with the groans and boos. Hanratty glared at his aide, who slumped in her seat.

"Meghan?" President Oobima pointed at a young CBS reporter. "Help Mr. Hanratty out."

"Ma'am, the martial law imposed by interim President Pillosi in January lasted 48 hours. Two days."

"Correct. President Pillosi imposed martial law to save Americans from other Americans. It was a brave call. The martial law imposed for 48 hours gave us all a chance to calm down. It was dark, it was cold, people were rioting in the streets, and President Trimp had just attempted to destroy Canada with nuclear weapons." The press corps folks shook their heads as if what President Oobima was reminding them of seemed long ago, unbelievable. "I know. It sounds crazy, doesn't it?" Michelle shook her head.

"So, let me keep going. This helps all of us remember where we've been lately. We have to learn from our recent history. Our recent history indicates that Trimp and his followers are relentless. Relentless in their pursuit of power.

"Six days after trying to nuke our northern neighbors, on 27 January 2020, Trimp is unlawfully freed from a psychiatric hospital, by force, and declares himself, illegally, to be the rightful POTUS. He places interim President Pillosi and her administration under arrest. He then declares martial law and suppresses free speech for 91 days. All the media not favorable to Trimp was suppressed for 91 days. All the TV networks except Fox were mysteriously disabled for 91 days. Newspapers were shut down. 91 days Sean." President Oobima was getting worked up now. Hanratty got up and left the room. His aide scampered after him. The president ignored him.

Michelle Oobima was on a roll. Her voice was crisp, sharp, angry. "Do you recall the Resistance Rallies? When Americans organised legal peaceful assemblies to protest against Trimp's illegal armed occupation of the White House? And to demand that the Independent People's

Party be allowed to enter candidates in our federal election? 2.6 million innocent Americans were imprisoned during that period of martial law. My husband and I and Barney Saunders and Vice President John-Stone, and some of you here today, and many of you watching at home were imprisoned illegally." Her voice went soft again.

"And some 27,200 Americans lost their lives during that period of martial law.

"But we didn't give up. Remember? Americans kept protesting. Our friends in the international community were protesting. 341 million people protested in a 24-hour rally held all over the world. The whole world applied pressure on Trimp. And on 28 April, after 91 days of illegally imposed martial law, he snapped under that pressure. We didn't. The American people didn't even bend." She said the last part in a snarl.

"That's when Trimp and his puppet master Vladimir Poutine got desperate. They tried to start a world war. They tried to attack our country with nuclear weapons hoping that America would unite behind Trimp as a wartime president. Worse yet, they even tried to make it look like North Korea attacked us. So, for the second time in 98 days, Trimp was again arrested. And interim President Pillosi was reinstated, again, as per our Constitution.

"We had an election in November, and the American people overwhelmingly voted for members of the

Independent People's Party..." President Oobima was cut off by journalists cheering. She blushed, but only for a brief moment.

"Thank you for that. During that election, interim President Pillosi requested 250,000 UN peacekeepers from Canada to assist with security during the election. Again, a very courageous decision. A very unpopular decision. Many Americans were embarrassed by this decision. Rightfully so. It's not normal that a functioning democracy needs UN peacekeepers to defend its citizens from other citizens with differing political views. But elected leaders often have to make unpopular decisions for the good of the majority of their citizens. There were intelligence reports from the CIA, FBI, Homeland Security, and many other security agencies that indicated Trimp supporters intended to harass and harm people exercising their democratic right to vote. Think about that for a minute. With Trimp in prison for the second time in six months, a small persistent percentage of our population intended to sway an election by any means: with fear and with violence."

Her voice went soft again. She had been on fire, eyes blazing, engaging everyone in the room. Now she just looked down. "Seven days after the election, with Trimp serving a life sentence for treason, armed Trimp supporters attacked us at Arlington on Veteran's Day. 68 people died." She went silent for a minute. The room was quiet.

The president lifted her head defiantly. "In the days and months that followed, there were many, many more attacks by hate groups," she said. "The violence even spread outside our borders, to Canada, to Europe. Violence and racism and hatred disguised as nationalism. We began to realise it wasn't about Trimp anymore," she said. "We suspected this years ago. 'Trimp is not the disease: Trimp is a symptom of the disease,' we said. Trimp is the figurehead, the mascot, the bombastic bullying face and voice of hatred and fear. We know that Trimp is not the disease because the Trimp cult carried on even during his incarceration. Even Trimp himself sees this now. Remember two nights ago when he said, 'even killing me won't kill me?'"

The journalists nodded. People watching the press conference at home nodded.

"'Even killing him won't kill him,'" she repeated. "What a sad, awful truth. We need to admit that this is a cult, with an insane Messiah. And now Donald Trimp is free once more. His followers are re-energised, and they want to see Trimp become the president once more. His followers have assembled in great numbers. They are banging their shields and waving their guns, and threatening to attack other Americans.

"I'm sorry my answer was so long. But I felt like we all needed a recap of where we've been. Once we recall where we've been, we can assess where we need to go.

"What am I prepared to do? Everything I must to protect Americans. Whatever it takes. Nothing is off the table. Now, please excuse me. I promise I will keep you updated as much as I can. Stay strong. Be good to each other."

***

CHAPTER 13.

To Stop Me: Open on Dotted Line

America

12-14 May 2021

For the next several days, the world watched on uneasily. The people who had been fleeing San Francisco, Baltimore, and Washington had returned home. They were now being joined by millions of people fleeing Trimpanzee gathering points. There were very few identifiable 'Libtards' or 'Snowflakes' left in Palm Beach, Dallas, Houston, or Phoenix. Non-Trimp supporters felt unsafe in those places and went to stay elsewhere with friends and relatives.

400,000 Americans applied for Canadian citizenship in the week following Trimp's release. Many tried to claim refugee status, arguing that their country was no longer safe to live in. Another 325,000 went to Panama, Mexico, or South America seeking safety. Others went to Italy, Ireland,

Spain, Portugal, New Zealand, and other safe-havens. Homes and businesses for sale in the former 'red' states skyrocketed, but nobody was buying. People who owned homes there were reluctantly renting them out to Trimp loyalists. Others who couldn't leave swallowed their pride and bought Trimp hats and shirts to avoid a beating.

On FOX, various Trimpanzees were celebrating their Messiah's recent pardon at large hate rallies.

Gladys Hanover from Biloxi looked just like anyone's regular Grandmother. If regular Grandmothers were bleached blondes wearing 'Proud Racist Bitch' T-shirts with a Trimp picture on the front, a Confederate flag on the Back, and swastikas on each sleeve. "Of course, I'm happy that the fake president pardoned President Trimp. She knew he was always innocent. Oh, by the way: Michelle: I've always known you were a man."

Joe Tippet from Tulsa seemed like a regular Joe if regular Joes enjoyed the idea of killing those with differing political views. "I'm disappointed that President Trimp didn't get to use his 'Space Weapon' on the Libs and Communists. We could Make America Greater Again, faster, without them. Time to start over with a clean slate, with Real Americans."

Chip Savage from Miami was easier to read than Gladys or Joe. Chip looked like the sort of man you might cross the street to avoid. He was shirtless and wore two bandoliers of ammo to feed a 50 calibre machine gun. He had multiple tattoos, all with violent graphics. On his left arm, a knife in a skull with 'Freedom Isn't Free' underneath it. On his right arm, he had some skeletons parachuting into a battle, guns blazing. 'Death from Above' was the slogan under that picture. The most striking or upsetting tattoo Chip sported was a dotted line that went ear to ear under his jawline. It read 'To Stop Me: Open on Dotted Line.'

Chip looked like a man who may have killed people with knives recently. He sounded crazier than he looked, even to veteran FOX viewers. "For any snowflakes, pussies, and liberal scum watching: I'm an Iraq war veteran with two tours of duty. Most of my friends are veterans. Everyone here is heavily armed. Most of you not loyal to President Trimp don't even know which f@#$ing bathroom to use. I see your impending deaths as a mercy killing. We do not need a 'Space Weapon' to send you to hell. Honestly, it'll be more fun killing you face to face. You might wanna skip your next few ballet classes and lift a few weights, or take a self defence course, buy a gun, and learn how to use it. You could also save my friends and me the trouble and take your own sorry lives now. I can't promise I'll be merciful when I kill you. Later pussies. Heil Trimp!"

Rick ended his monologue with a Nazi salute. As the camera panned out, viewers could see many of Rick's friends in the crowd returning the salute.

"What is Trimp doing now that he's free?" people wondered.

According to the 'Lamestream Media,' Trimp spent his time golfing, hate tweeting, eating hamberders, and meeting with his henchmen.

"So, the same stuff he did while he was president?"

There were rumours on the gossip shows he was banging his spiritual advisor Paulette White, or Tommi Lauren, or both. The same gossip shows were doing follow-ups on Melanie and Barron.

Melanie had returned to Slovenia after Trimp's second arrest and taken Barron and her parents with her. "And quite a bit of Trimp's dwindling fortune as well," chuckled the talking gossip heads. Melanie was doing some TV work as the voice of a cartoon vampire on a popular Slovenian children's show. She was also co-authoring a book with Marley Maples and Ivana Trimp, two of Donald's other ex-wives. The "Ex Factors" had already presold a million copies.

If you switched back to FOX, coverage was different again. President Trimp was busy meeting with other heads of state and planning his second inauguration. "I've got a great team, and we are going to Make America Great Again. Believe me; it's gonna be even greater than before," he told Sean Hanratty.

***

UN Headquarters, Geneva

For the second time in six months, Elijah presented a peacekeeping proposal to the United Nations Security Council. It was premised on the assumption that the United States would soon be engulfed in a civil war. The Canadian government suggested that peacekeepers could be essential in preventing that war from escalating. The proposal was submitted with the full support of President Oobima's administration.

The resolution proposed that 50,000 Canadian peacekeepers be surged into the US every two days, up to a maximum of 400,000. They would be housed and quartered at American military bases or in stadiums and arenas refitted as temporary housing.

The resolution passed unanimously.

Over the past two years, the Canadian military had been training for missions exactly like this: aid to the civil power, disaster relief, peacekeeping, and security operations. They had been deployed to the 49th parallel during the Great Canadian Blackout and as peacekeepers during the last US election.

"Sir: the last time you sent peacekeeping troops into America, our soldiers were unarmed. Will these troops be armed?

"Yes." The Canadian prime minister was famous for answering questions directly.

Are you concerned about sending troops trained for peacekeeping into a hostile situation in America? This is gonna be a full out war, not a peacenik convention," a journalist from *The Maple Leaf* shouted.

"OK- stop," he said, pointing angrily at the offending journalist. "That's a ridiculous statement. Stop trying to scare people for a clickbait article. The members of our military are very well trained. The troops who deploy will all be experienced volunteers. No one will be forced to go. This is not a war; it's a peacekeeping operation in a neighboring country, with whom we share a long border. We also have a tremendous relationship and a shared history with our American neighbors."

"We had a tremendous relationship with America," the journalist persisted. "But you're sending our troops into a potential war zone, where angry supporters of their former president will see the presence of peacekeepers as an insult to their pride. Can you promise Canadians their sons and daughters won't be hurt or killed?"

"No."

"Then why send them?" the reporter persisted.

"Because it's the right thing to do." Elijah snapped back. "Because we still care. Because peacekeepers can make a positive difference in situations like this. Because

60 years ago, Canadians invented peacekeeping, and we're really, really good at it. Since that time, peacekeepers have saved millions of lives in hundreds of conflicts. I'm one of those lives. Put my story in your column. Tell people how Canadian peacekeepers rescued 125 other child soldiers and me in Somalia. Three of those peacekeepers died to win our freedom. Tell that story, and then equate it to the current mission, and let your readers decide if peacekeeping is a worthy cause."

The press scrum went quiet.

***

Niagara Falls

Cpl. Lumpy Halerewich was running his platoon through masking drills.

"This gas mask will protect you in a nuclear, biological, or chemical environment. You need to be able to put this mask on in nine seconds. When you have reason to believe that a threat is present: you see smoke, you see vapor, you smell something different: hold your breath, close your eyes, yell: GAS, GAS GAS to warn others, then mask up. When your mask is secure, breathe out hard to clear your mask of whatever agent may have fallen in the mask. Do you understand?"

"Yes, Cpl." Three Platoon responded.

"How's this training going, Cpl. Halerewich?" Sergeant Major Lee asked. Father Jakub, the Padre, was with her.

Apparently, the question was rhetorical. Before Halerewich could answer, Sgt. Major Lee threw a smoke grenade into the room that started spinning around on the floor, billowing yellow smoke. She smiled sweetly at the startled troops, clicked a stopwatch, held her breath, and put on her gas mask. She tightened the straps and checked her seal. She exhaled twice sharply.

Five Seconds. God, I love this shit, she thought to herself.

"GAS! GAS! GAS!" Halerewich shouted at his troops. As the tiny sgt. major looked on; she made mental notes. *Very few eyes closed. Most troops are not holding their breath. One panicking and putting the mask on upside down. Masks not in gas mask pouches according to SOP. Two trying to suck in air through rubber seal still on the canister, one mask without a canister? Three troops with masks on who didn't tighten straps and check seal acting cocky like they've done it right... Father Jakub, well, I'll talk to him after, privately.*

She glanced at the stopwatch. Thirty seconds. She removed her mask.

"Stop! Stand still! Don't move!" she screamed. All of her troops described her angry voice slightly differently. Some said "it was like a whip cracking or a pistol shot." "Her voice has a sharp edge, like jagged glass dipped in poison that you know will hurt you badly," said others.

"But she only uses that voice when we're maggoty," they agreed.

"I said stand still, you horrible little man," she screamed in the face of a private who was still struggling with his mask. The kid froze.

"I'm going to take a moment and debrief you all. First, let me congratulate you on your uniformity." She paused. "You're all dead." She paused again.

"Not one of you put on the C5 mask within the allotted time within the standard required to keep you alive. If that smoke grenade contained a nerve, chemical, or biological agent, you'd all be dead. If the canister had been a harassing agent like mustard gas, tear gas, or pepper spray, 90 percent of you would now be useless as soldiers: crying, choking, and blind. I'm going to speak to each of you in turn and tell you what I saw.

"Halerewich. You did almost everything right. You held your breath, raised the alarm, and got your mask on in seven seconds, but your eyes were open the whole time, looking at your troops. So regardless of the agent, you're blinded, at least for a few minutes."

"Thank you, Sgt. Major," Halerwich shouted through his mask.

"Don't thank me, you sightless lummox. Go stand in that corner by the window," Sgt. Major Lee said.

"MacDaw and Rempert?"

"Yes, Sgt. Major?" MacDaw and Rempert were really struggling to breathe.

"Are you having trouble breathing through your mask?"

"Yes, Sgt. Major!" The two confirmed.

"MacDaw and Rempert only, unmask!" she shouted.

The two privates ripped off their masks and gasped for air. "Hold out your masks," the sgt. major said. The two complied. "Tip your masks over at a 45-degree angle to the right. Do you see a rubber plug on the outside of that filter that might impede your breathing?" Both privates nodded, blushing. "Remove the rubber plug, and put it in your mask carrying case." The two complied, still blushing.

"MacDaw; explain to your platoon the function of the rubber plug."

"Sgt. Major, we put the plug in place when the mask is in a long period of storage to avoid getting moisture in the canister or filter."

"Indeed. Rempert: when we know that the mask is likely to be required for training or - God forbid- a real emergency, what should be done with the rubber plug?"

"Sgt. Major, we should remove the plug and put it in the gas mask carrying case."

"Good explanation. MacDaw and Rempert only. Put your masks back in the gas mask carrying case. Close the case. MacDaw and Rempert only: "GAS! GAS! GAS!" The two privates re-masked. "Too slow, eyes not closed, straps not tightened, seal not tested. Rempert: don't keep breathing. As soon as you hear gas, hold your breath. Keep your masks on. Go lay on the floor by the door. You're both dead."

Sgt. Major Lee moved quickly from soldier to soldier and explained to each of them why they were dead or blind. She saved Pte Mullins for her last review.

"Mullins: how do you think you did?" the miniature sgt. major asked in a friendly tone.

"Well, I held my breath, and closed my eyes, and got the mask on quick, tightened my straps, blew out two times quick, and checked my seal. I think I did good, Sgt. Major." Mullins replied nervously, in the muffled tones of a young lady wearing a C5 gas mask.

"That's all true, Mullins. But there's one important thing missing."

Mullins looked curious.

"Put your hand in your mask carrying case. Pull out that round, lumpy thing that's hermetically sealed at tremendous expense to the Canadian taxpayer."

Mullins did as directed and looked like she wanted to die or cry or disappear when she saw what she was holding.

"Read to me what that is, Mullins."

"Ch ...charcoal activated filter for use on the C5 Gas mask..."

"And where should that charcoal activated filter be, Mullins?"

"Fitted onto my gas mask, Sgt. Major." Mullins looked like she was ready to cry.

"Unmask and put that filter on Mullins."

The 23 dead people lying on the floor and 3 blind people standing by the door started to laugh. The sgt. major wheeled on them like a little Tasmanian devil. "Shut your dead maggoty cake holes," she shouted. "Dead people can't laugh at other dead people. And it was a visual moment, so none of you people blinded by tear gas saw it either. I made exactly that same mistake 22 years ago when I was in recruit training. We're all human. We can all make mistakes. Mullins: now that you've got your filter on your mask, you'll be fine. You were the only one who did the drill by the book. Just the fairly significant matter of a missing filter, which is now rectified." Sgt. Major Lee let the platoon think about that for a minute.

"Halerewich?"

"Yes, Sgt. Major?"

"I have just miraculously given sight back to your sightless troops and resurrected your dead. Not out of sympathy or compassion. I just don't want their corpses to stink up my Armory. Get these people up, put them back in three ranks, at open order formation, and order them to unmask, then stand them back at attention."

Sgt. Major Lee stepped back and looked out a window at other troops doing circuit training. When they were back at attention, she wheeled about.

"Stand at ease. Stand easy," she barked. The platoon relaxed in place, or as much as you can relax in the company of an unpredictable sgt. major. "We leave for Miami in 36 hours," she said quietly. "It is my job to ensure I bring as many of you back as I can. I detest writing letters that say: *'Dear Mr. and Mrs. Bloggins, I regret to inform you that I did not train your son or daughter to the best of my abilities, etc., etc., thoughts and prayers.'* She paced back and forth as she spoke.

"I will not apologise for training you to a high standard. I will not apologise for calling you maggots when you behave like maggots. You should never think that I dislike you, personally, more than any other maggots because that would indicate prejudice on my part. Therefore, I shall dislike you all equally until the entire group of you becomes proficient in all things soldierly. Halerewich, take them for a run around the perimeter of the armory, inside the fence, full battle dress, weapons, and helmets."

Sgt. Major Lee stepped back as Cpl. Halerewich got them ready to roll. As they marched out the door, she noticed Mullins had a spring in her step.

"That was a nice touch with Pte. Mullins," Father Yakub said quietly. "She's very timid and easily ...bruised? Is that the right word?" He'd been standing in the corner quietly the whole time.

"Well, most times they need a kick in the ass, and occasionally they need to hear that they did well."

"It's nice to see. They know that deep down, you love them, Sgt. Major," Father Jakub joked.

"Let's not get carried away, Padre. Let me show you something I noticed while we did the drill. Take out your mask."

Sgt. Major Lee patiently explained: "loosen these straps, and put the mask in the gas mask pouch like this, filter up. Watch me. When you need the mask, you can quickly pull it out by the filter, slide both thumbs under these straps, insert your chin, pull the mask over your head, then tighten straps, exhale hard twice, then check to ensure your mask has a proper seal." Sgt. Major Lee did it in slow time, then fast time. "Now, you. Gas! Gas! Gas!

Father Yakub masked and unmasked a few more times. "You've got this Padre," the sgt. major said. "Ooooh, here they are. Watch."

The platoon was just running by the open window. She pulled the wick on a smoke grenade and threw it ahead of the platoon. She stepped out the door into the bright sunlight. Smiling.

Father Jakub could still hear the sgt. major as he walked back to his office.

He had to ensure all the soldier's files contained a valid updated will.

***

CHAPTER 14.

Father Jakub's Other Job

Washington

The day after the UN agreed to send peacekeepers to the United States, 413 Americans were killed in clashes. Michelle Oobima met with her administration to discuss options.

Phyliss Brown was the new director of Homeland Security. She was a former army reserve colonel who had previously been in charge of the Illinois National Guard. Her background was in military intelligence and psychological operations.

"Ma'am, our intel indicates that armed conflict between the left and right is only going to escalate. The Trimp loyalists are heavily armed, upset, and lashing out. Many people fearing violence from a Trimp supporter have gone on the offensive, a 'kill or be killed' mentality. We've had sniper fire, running gun battles through neighborhoods, and all sorts of IED's. In between the Trimp loyalists and the people fighting them, we've got folks just trying to live their lives. Martial law is really the only way to keep people safe. Declaring martial law will allow us to calm things down on both sides. It will let us establish parameters: it will let us tell citizens what they can and cannot do. For example, we could suspend the right for Americans to bear arms outside of their own property: no more concealed carry, no more people shopping at WilMart with 2 assault rifles slung over their backs. Under martial law, we could declare a ceasefire and slow this down. Most importantly, after declaring martial law, our military will have the power to arrest and detain those who break the law."

"What are the possible negatives if we declare martial law?"

"Ma'am, the people who love guns also love their second amendment right to bear arms. Any attempt to constrain that right under the rule of martial law will be taken as an affront to the Constitution."

"Chief of Staff? Thoughts?" the president asked.

"Madam President, the director's points are valid. Martial law will give us a chance to create an 'area of separation' between the two factions. It would allow for the evacuation of personnel who don't want to be in the middle of either camp. However, even if we declare martial law and implement stricter gun control, most people who have guns won't want to give them up. Any police force, troops or peacekeepers we put in between the factions would be at significant risk."

"How do we minimize that risk? Is there a way?"

"Yes, Ma'am, we think there is. It's an idea we've been working on for a year or two in research and development, but we couldn't quite make it work. When we took control of the 'Space Force' satellite a few days ago, we found some technology there that will let us disarm everybody without hurting anyone. Would you like to see how it works?"

***

Miami Beach

The 500 soldiers of the Niagara Battalion flew into Homestead Air Reserve Base in Miami between 0800 and 0900. They arrived in 20 de Haviland Otters, 25 troops per plane. The Otters were a tough little bush plane first used in the 1950s to open up Canada's north. These were a new version of that same design. Four Canadian factories were building them, each producing about a thousand per year. The end goal was to produce 15,000 planes and have 45,000 people qualify as pilots to fly them.

To the American air traffic controllers, the Otters looked like a World War Two scene in the sky. The little two prop planes were white, festooned with red maple leaves. They were each flying about five kilometres or two minutes behind the plane in front of them. From the ground, it looked pretty curious.

"They don't have jets in Canada?" a young controller asked his captain. "What is this?"

The captain laughed. "These are little twin-prop Otters. There's a smaller version that seats 12. When we get them on the ground, go have a look. My Dad flew one of the originals in the '60s: he was a guide at a Minnesota fishing camp. These little planes will still be flying in 50 years."

The Otters only needed about five percent of the runway to land. They were being taxied into a line, where they would be refueled and head home again. As the soldiers deplaned, they were directed into a big hangar near the airstrip.

The American aircrew and pilots were amazed by the Otters and crowded around the planes, talking to the pilots.

"Sir, these planes are sick! It's like you took a plane from the 1950s and rebuilt it."

"That's exactly what we did. They're fun to fly," Father Jakub said, extending his hand. "Hey, I'm Jakub."

"Eric. Welcome to Miami. Sorry, it's such a shitshow here right now; we're all pretty embarrassed." Other pilots and crew were gathering around the Otter.

"Don't be embarrassed; we're just neighbours helping neighbours," Jakub replied kindly.

A group of young American techs had completed their circle of the plane. "Sir is there a weapons system onboard, or...?"

Jakub smiled. "Just on a few models, and it's pretty old school. We're gonna demo that now, in fact, but you can't laugh. See those last two planes?" As Jakub looked up, so did the others.

The last two Otters were up much higher than the others. Almost on cue, soldiers began spilling out the jump door. Within three minutes, there were 50 parachutes in the air.

Eric was grinning. "You're right. That is pretty old school. So you guys just use these for transport?"

"Pretty much. Last week we flew in firefighters and then evacuated some people from a fire in Alberta. The week before, we took a medical team and a MASH unit to a remote community up north. There are 200 bigger models we use as water bombers. So far, we've only used these planes for humanitarian missions, disaster relief, aid to civil power roles, and troop insertions like this."

"But Sir, what if there's a war? Wouldn't you rather have jets with smart bombs and missiles?" the young tech persisted.

Jakub smiled again. "Well, our government did the math on that a few years back. We had enough money to buy 50 F-35's..."

"Whoooooooo! That's what I'm talking bout. Now that's a kick-ass jet!" the young tech hooted.

"I ...guess," Jakub shrugged. "But jets are stupidly expensive, and all they can do is kick ass. These planes are useful all the time. We use them to help people. For the price of one F-35, we can build 300 of these little workhorses. I hope we never need to, but apparently, these can be fitted with a 50 calibre machine gun. We're building 15,000 of these, so in a dogfight, who'd win? An F-35, or 30 of these with 50 cals?" It was hot on the tarmac. As Jakub spoke, he unzipped his flight jacket and peeled out of it. "I'd bet on 30 of these," he said, patting the little Otter.

"You're a padre and a pilot?" said Eric, looking at Jakub's collar and the cross on his epaulettes.

"I'm sorry, Father," the young tech said, blushing. "I never meant to..." he trailed off.

"S'all good, relax," Jakub laughed. "We hear questions like yours at airbases all over the world. Canada is a big country, but we have a small population. So we need to get the most bang for our buck we can from equipment and people. A lot of us pull double duty. Like our sergeant major here just landing." Father Jakub pointed at Sgt. Major Lee. "She's an OR nurse in her off-duty hours."

The airfield watched as the paratroopers started landing on the grassy strip. Sgt. Major Lee stuck her landing like a pro. A minute later, Lumpy bounced off the side of a dome-shaped hangar and landed on his face on the tarmac. It was a pretty ugly landing. He wasn't moving. Father Jakub and two Americans ran over to him.

"Don't touch him," shouted the sergeant major as she ran over. "Let me check him first. He might have hurt his neck or spine; if we move him, it could make it worse," she explained calmly as she checked him over for injuries.

Lumpy started to stir. "Don't move, lummox," the sergeant major barked at him, "or I'll knock you out again. Let me finish checking you over."

"Yes, Sgt. Major," Lumpy replied, with his face in the asphalt.

"Where does it hurt?"

"My pride?" Lumpy groaned. The growing crowd around him smirked a little.

Sgt. Major Lee quickly ran him through some tests. "Wiggle your fingers. Now squeeze my finger. Again. Other hand. Can you wiggle your toes? Push against my hand with your foot. Now this way. Count backwards by sevens from 99."

"99, 92, um 85...."

"That's enough. I don't think you could do that before you hit your head. I also don't think you're seriously hurt. Can you roll over, or do you want help?"

"I can do it, Sgt. Major." Lumpy rolled over and blushed at the crowd. The crowd applauded as he sat up. "Sgt. Major?"

"Yes?"

"Why the counting test? Isn't that for Alzheimer's patients?"

"Yes, normally. I thought maybe you had Alzheimer's because you forgot everything you were taught at jump school." The crowd chuckled more easily now as Lumpy seemed to have no lasting damage. "For all future jumps, try to avoid buildings, trees, and rivers. And try landing on your feet for once."

"Hey, is Fabiola, I mean, Pte. Gonzalez on the ground yet?" Lumpy enquired, looking around for his girlfriend.

"Here she comes now," said Lumpy's buddy T-Bone.

Fabiola nailed the landing, rolled, and picked up her chute in one efficient motion.

"I'm just glad she didn't see my landing," Lumpy said.

"Dude, it's already got over 900 likes on Instagram," T-Bone teased him, holding up his phone. "Do you remember it?"

"I remember thinking it was gonna hurt...but then, yeah, nothing."

T-Bone handed Lumpy his phone. "Here, check it out. Duder, it's sickening. Listen to the crunch when your brain bucket hits the runway..."

"Hey, what did I miss? Is everybody good?" Fabiola asked.

"Your boyfriends a celebrity," the sergeant major told Fabiola dryly. "All right everybody: shows over." The crowd applauded as Lumpy got up, beet red with embarrassment.

Then in her scary sergeant major voice: "Niagaras: get your slack and idle carcasses in that hanger. We have a briefing in five minutes."

"Thank goodness I didn't have to do my other job," Father Jakub said as he drifted back to his plane.

The American pilots looked at him curiously.

"You know, last rites or a funeral."

***

CHAPTER 15.

Proud Racist Bitch

America

The civil unrest raged on. There had been no formal declaration of war by Congress; hence the term 'civil unrest' was being used by the government and most media.

Some Trimp supporters were referring to the unrest as a 'Holy War,' led by God's President, Donald Trimp. The religious among them eagerly anticipated that 'The Rapture' would occur after their victory. The other more violent faction of Trimp supporters didn't care what the unrest was called. They just wanted to lash out, hurt, and kill libtards, snowflakes, foreigners, persons of color, and socialists: essentially anyone not like them. Trimp, meanwhile, spent his time golfing and tweeting nonsense. Like this:

@RealDonaldTrimp: sorry (not sorry) about all the Liberal deaths lately. FAKE PRESIDENT Michelle, you have the power to make it stop! Resign, proclaim me as the rightful PRESIDENT of the USA. Crooked Mallory: you started this when you called us DEPLORABLES! #MAGA #KAG #LOCKHERUP

Numerous panels of famous psychologists on various channels (not FOX) pointed out that this absolute chaos and hatred was Trimp's version of heaven. "He could not be any happier than he is right now," agreed the mental health experts. "He desperately needs attention, and the whole world is watching him. He loves the battles and infighting, and he gets an adrenaline rush like a cocaine addict watching people fight. He takes his greatest joy in the suffering and pain of his perceived enemies. It's not enough for Trimp to win the fight. He needs his enemies to be debased, degraded, tortured, humiliated, torn asunder, resurrected, re-assembled, and tortured some more."

"Don't forget, this is a man who raised his children with the mantra: 'when someone hurts you, hurt them back ten times harder,'" added a doctor from Johns Hopkins.

Each day the death toll climbed: 661, 1043, 2045, then 4002 lives were lost. About double that number were injured each day. The Never Trimper's blamed the Trimpanzees for starting the violence. The Trimpanzees blamed the socialist snowflake libtards. Meanwhile, looters took advantage of empty homes and businesses. Pandemonium.

After three days of fiery, passionate deliberation in Congress, martial law was approved. Most independents and most democrats voted in favor. Nine democrats and all the republican representatives voted against the resolution.

The following day, at 0800 hours Eastern Standard Time, President Michelle Oobima signed the resolution and declared martial law. This declaration of martial law came with specific provisions:

1. Members of the United States Armed Forces are hereby given authority to search property without warrants and to arrest and detain citizens committing unlawful acts in accordance with the provisions of this declaration.

2. This declaration of martial law supersedes state and municipal laws pertaining to firearms. No civilian citizen shall carry a firearm outside of their private property.

3. Gun owners not currently in their homes have 48 hours to turn in their weapons at local police stations or return to their homes. The weapons voluntarily turned in will be returned to citizens when the declaration of martial law is lifted and when those citizens have returned to their homes.

4. Citizens apprehended with firearms who are not on their own property will be arrested, and their weapons will be forfeited.

5. For their own safety, citizens are to remain in their homes during this declaration. Police and military personnel will operate checkpoints. Citizens will be allowed to travel to medical appointments, grocery stores, pharmacies, and work.

6. Citizens must carry and present government photo identification when outside their private property...

The list of provisions went on, but the first four were the ones that really upset people who had 'from my cold dead hands' T-shirts and bumper stickers.

The declaration of martial law and the provisions regarding firearms from President Oobima opened floodgates of violence. Historians later agreed that it was indeed a civil war; it only lacked a formal declaration of war against a common enemy.

***

Homestead Air Reserve Base

At Homestead and military bases all across the US, Canadian peacekeepers and US military personnel were training for crowd control. Lumpy, T-Bone, Fabiola, and the Niagara Regiment learned how to use a new taser with a plastic base. As part of their training, they each had to get zapped by a partner. They were supposed to use the low setting. T-Bone and Lumpy volunteered to get zapped on the high setting, much to all the trainee's delight. They did multiple gas mask drills, as they were almost certain that tear gas and smoke would be necessary to subdue and disarm the crowd. They worked on vehicle search techniques, looking for bombs and other weapons. Door kicking and search techniques were refined and improved. The troops practised in close formation with shields and riot sticks and with mounted police on horseback. They practised the proper and safest technique to control and zap strap someone without getting knifed, shot, or hurt. There were briefings to discuss the establishment and maintenance of Areas of Separation (AOS). Rules of Engagement (ROE) were learned and relearned. Miranda rights and the legal rights of detainees and soldiers were memorized. Firefighting and first aid training were refreshed. The training was exhausting and challenging, but also satisfying.

43 hours after the declaration of Martial Law, at 0400 hours, Lieutenant - Colonel Melissa Brown of the United States Army addressed the troops in a large hangar. The combined American and Canadian troops had formed a good bond over the four days of training.

"I've enjoyed watching you train together these past days," she said. "I know the pace of this training was relentless. It had to be. Our country is in trouble, and we need to create Areas of Separation between these two factions. Yesterday some 13,000 Americans were killed as a result of this infighting." She paused to give the troops time to digest that number. "The worst of it has been happening here in Miami because of its proximity to Mar-a-Lago, where Trimp is located.

"We're about to discuss a new tactic we haven't trained for yet. But first, raise your hand if you have a cell phone," she said in a friendly tone, "cuz I need someone to take a picture for me." No one budged.

"Good. If you raised your hand there, I might have broken it for you." Now, raise your hand if you turned in your cell phones last Saturday night at 2100 hours." 1000 hands were raised.

"Very good. I want to remind y'all why no one has a cell phone. Cell phones can be distracting, and we need you focused. Cell phones have cameras that people sometimes use to take hero photos or action shots of operations. Not on my watch. With a cell phone, you could knowingly or unknowingly leak information about our location or tactics to someone who might use that information against us. As of last Saturday, this unit and many others across our country have been on comms lockdown. HUA?" she shouted.

"HooooooWahhhhhhhhh!" a thousand voices responded in unison.

Heard. Understood. Acknowledged.

"Alright. Let's talk tactics. First. We will NOT be using standard military weapons on this operation."

The assembled troops began to chatter. "WTF did she just ...?"

"Shut your pie holes and listen," snapped Sergeant Major Lee. The hangar went quiet.

"Thank you, Sgt. Major," Lt. Col. Brown replied graciously. "As I was saying, we will NOT be using standard firearms during this op..."

***

Mar-a-Lago

At 0500, the Canadian and American troops were loaded into deuce and a half trucks, Armoured Personnel Carriers, and buses. They had nicknamed themselves 'The Devil's Brigade,' after a legendary brigade of Canadians and Americans that fought with distinction in Italy during WW II.

The Devil's Brigade drove up I-95 north from the Homestead Base, with 2 APC's leading. Lumpy counted 35 golf courses between Miami Beach and Palm Beach. They went by three airports, which were lit up, but there were no flights. At the Palm Beach Zoo, they turned right onto a causeway that crossed a lagoon. By 0545, they had formed a human perimeter around the beachfront of Mar-a-Lago. It was still dark. They waited.

"It's so quiet," Lumpy whispered to Fabiola.

"Not for long," she whispered back.

At 0600, just as dawn was breaking, Lieutenant -Colonel Brown gave a signal. One of the APC's fired up a deafening air raid siren. 'The Devils' could hear multiple similar sirens on the other 3 sides of Trimp's property. The sirens wailed for 30 seconds. Armed security personnel from Team America spilled out from the guest residences and the Southern White House. Trimpanzees in the Mar-a-Lago hotel looked out windows, many with rifles hastily pointed out windows at the unarmed troops. Other guests were joining Team America outside. They were half asleep, bewildered, angry.

"This is Lieutenant - Colonel Brown of the United States Army," a megaphone blared. "This operation is sanctioned by martial law. My troops are unarmed. Drop your weapons, NOW!"

Team America and the angry Trimpanzees responded as one.

"Ready!"

"Aim!"

"Fire!" a Team America captain yelled. Click. Click. "What the actual F#$%?"

The troops drew a breath. *Glad that worked as advertised* is what most of the soldiers recalled thinking later.

Trimp's loyalists were befuddled. Their weapons would not fire. They were racking actions, and pulling triggers repeatedly, and reloading with different magazines, and then pulling out pistols that also wouldn't fire. They were confused, cursing, spitting mad.

"GAS! GAS! GAS!" the megaphone blared. 'The Devil's' put on their masks. A few seconds later, the gas canisters were falling among Team America and the Trimpanzees. Seconds later, the troops fired canisters through each hotel window.

"Devil's, by the centre, QUICK MARCH," Lieutenant Colonel Brown shouted to her troops. The Devil's Brigade moved forward slowly in one unbroken line as they had trained. Each soldier was touching the shoulder of the person beside them. They had been numbered and partnered: one-two, one-two. Every number one soldier had a Plexiglas shield and a riot stick. With every pace on their left foot, they rapped the riot stick on the shield. Every number two soldier had a taser and zap straps.

A few of the Trimpanzees were running away from the troops, which was a bad idea. The gentle morning breeze was blowing the tear gas that way. Some members of Team America were former military members and police officers who had been released for crimes. Others were never deemed suitable for government service. They did have some experience in quelling crowds. Nine months ago, they had held all the cards. During the 'Resistance Rallies', Team America had gassed, clubbed, and brutally arrested 2.6 million citizens protesting against Trimp. The Team America captain rallied his troops, and with several hundred enraged Trimpanzees by their side, they rushed the troops. They wielded their rifles like clubs now, screaming, cursing with rage, choking, nearly blind.

The troops pressed forward slowly. As their charging opponents came within 5 metres, or 15 feet, they were tased. Being gassed sucks enough. Being tased after being gassed really sucks. Being tased makes you lose control of your muscles for about nine seconds. 80% of the Trimpanzees went down and started twitching, which is the taser's desired effect. Some of the more stubborn people needed 2 or 3 zaps before they went down. The line stayed together, stepping over the first group of twitching Trimpanzees.

The second wave of Devil's in the same formation as the first moved behind the first line. They worked together as one unit, zapping and strapping the Trimp loyalists: faces down with hands behind their backs. One large man in garish Team America camouflage regained his feet and pulled a Bowie knife from his boot. He was about to bury the knife in Fabiola's back when three soldiers tased him. Lumpy knocked him out with his riot stick for good measure.

In nine minutes, they had rounded up the strays. They were drug together into one pile of 437 angry Trimp loyalists. "Stay still and relax," they were told. "If you move, we'll tase you again." Only a stubborn few needed extra tasing.

The large angry guy who tried to stab Fabiola got another tasing and clubbing. An American female soldier was giving people in distress sips of water when he kicked her viciously in the face. Once subdued, they zap strapped his feet, flipped him on his stomach, and strapped his feet to his hands behind his back. He kept raging and saying awful things, so he was gagged for good measure. He had a weird neck tattoo with dots like a box top. It read: To Stop Me: Open On Dotted Line.

"There's an order I'd love to follow," said the young soldier who had been kicked in the face.

Most of the maids, cleaners, servers, cooks, and a few guests had come out of the hotel peacefully, with arms raised and surrendered. The first lady was zap strapped to a fence. The rest were zap strapped by one hand to the person beside them. "Is it OK if we smoke?" a gardener asked Fabiola.

"Give the gas a few minutes to clear out," she replied cheerfully in Spanish. "As long as the people near you don't mind? Ask them. Everybody relax; we're trying not to hurt anyone who has peacefully surrendered," she continued, still in Spanish. Winston Wee, a Chinese Canadian soldier, repeated the same message in Mandarin and English.

An angry-looking older blonde female guest demanded loudly that "I will not be handcuffed to a Chink, a Nigger, or a Mexican."

"Yes, Ma'am," Fabiola said sweetly. "As you wish." Then she tasered her and zap strapped her hands behind her back. "Stay face down and don't move, or I'll taser you till your 'Proud Racist Bitch' heart stops," Fabiola whispered in her ear.

Lieutenant -Colonel Brown pointed the megaphone at the hotel. "You people in the hotel, come out peacefully, starting with the first floor. Bring your room key. When you exit your room, leave the door open. Use the stairs, not the elevator."

Most occupants came willingly. Out of 1200 guests, 237 had to be convinced to leave. The most inventive of them had assembled in a big group on the top floor and sprayed the troops with fire hoses. The troops backed away and down a floor for two minutes, and the Trimpanzees cheered their victory.

"This is Sgt. Washington. We have anybody in the mechanical room?" he asked into a two-way radio.

"Yes, sarge. This is Blackmore and Espinoza. What do you need?"

"Cut the power and the water to the top floor, and then turn on the sprinkler system."

"Roger that sgt. It'll take a couple of minutes for the sprinklers to drain the system after I cut the water."

"A couple of minutes is fine," Washington replied calmly. He was an older black man, more salt than pepper in his hair, probably closer to 60 than 50, lean and tough. He switched channels and spoke briefly to the lieutenant-colonel. Twenty seconds later, he smiled as the troops watched another volley of tear gas go in through the top floor windows.

"That gas is waaaaay worse when you're wet," he chuckled to the Devil's in the stairwell with him. "Now these people are gonna be upset." The soldiers could hear the Trimpanzees coughing, choking, and screaming. "We should start to see them shortly," he said. Now the troops could hear the trimpanzees near the door to the stairs.

"Here's a line I always wanted to say." He paused for dramatic effect. "Set your phasers on stun." The Devil's looked at him blankly. Most of them were under 22 years of age.

"What?"

"Y'all never saw Star Trek? Never mind. Get ready. Same as before. Zap strap the willing. Taser the other assholes till they are willing."

Most were compliant. Washington was right; the gas was more effective on wet people. They were in rough shape. The gas droplets clung to their wet clothing and skin. The last five holdouts were the toughest. They had wrapped their heads and faces in towels to minimize the effect of the gas. They tried to bust out as a group. They had armed themselves with CO_2 fire extinguishers, which they aimed at Sergeant Washington and his troops. Thankfully, the tasers had a slightly longer range.

Like the gas, the tasing seemed to be more effective on wet people. They were twitching and hollering more than normal. But wet people holding metal fire extinguishers? Holding something metal while being wet intensified the electrical shock capacity of the taser.

Back on the ground nine minutes later, Lieutenant-Colonel Brown called it in on her 2-way radio. "Romeo One, this is Delta Four. Objective achieved. Grid Tango Seven is secure. We have 1504 total detainees. Currently conducting perimeter searches and ensuring our detainees stay healthy. We are stockpiling weapons. We await further instructions. Over."

The radio was choppy and static-filled for a minute. "Uhhhh, copy that Delta Four. Take 500 of your people to Grid Tango Eight, beachside, and assist Delta Three.

"Romeo One, Copy that." She checked her map. The next grid was Trimp's residence, the fabled 'Southern White House.' She conferred quickly with her Canadian counterpart, then picked up her megaphone.

***

CHAPTER 16.

Stiff as a Mackerel

Washington, The White House Bunker

"Madam President, as of 1000 hours this morning, we are getting good early reports across most regions," the Chief of Joint Staff was saying, using a laser pointer to highlight graphs and charts.

"Under the provisions of martial law, we have arrested some 2.3 million persons, and early estimates suggest almost triple that number of firearms. Detainees are being processed and held in stadiums, arenas, and public buildings. The peacekeepers who initially assisted with arrests are transitioning into the delivery of humanitarian aid: food, water, and medical care to our detainees."

"And Trimp?"

"Yes, Ma'am. His security forces put up significant resistance this morning at Mar-a Lago. Still, they were all eventually subdued and arrested. Trimp and some 50 of his closest advisors hid inside a bunker. They were eventually driven out with tear gas and thunderflashes. We have footage. Would you like to..."

"Yes, please. There is nothing I'd rather see this morning more than Donald Trimp being arrested. Again," Michelle Oobima said.

The footage began by showing a fairly fierce battle between Team America personnel and Florida police. The police used the same tactic as the military: troops shoulder to shoulder. Odd numbers get a shield and riot baton. Even numbers get a taser. The Team America personnel at least put up a good fight. Trimp, his sons, and closest friends were enraged, crying for lawyers.

"Your lawyers right here," one police sergeant said to Trimp, pointing at a comatose and grey Rudy Ghouliani. No one had seen Rudy move in months. He just kept showing up wherever Trimp was in a wheelchair with oxygen bottles.

"Is this guy even still alive?" a junior police officer asked the sergeant.

"Great question. Take a pulse."

"Nope. Nothing. He's stiff as a mackerel Sarge and twice as cold. This guy has been dead for a couple of days."

"Get a medic to confirm that..."

"That's enough," President Oobima said. "What's our best estimate for our people to finish this op?"

"Ma'am, we're optimistic that we can be finished by 1800 hours tonight."

"Very impressive. Let me know if anything changes. I'll work on the next steps."

"Aye aye, Madam President." The Joint Chiefs stood as one and saluted Michelle as she left the room.

***

At 1750 hours Atlantic Standard Time, somebody somewhere flipped a switch. The internet worked. Well, sort of partially. Electrical power was restored. Lights, fridges, TVs, radios, and computers suddenly came to life. Cars could start. A hardcore Trimpist realised that guns worked again and murdered seven Americans of Mexican ancestry in rural Texas two minutes later.

"President Oobima will address the nation at 1800 hours AST," was the message on every computer screen, cellphone and radio via the Emergency Broadcast System.

As advertised, precisely at 1800 hours, President Oobima began her address. It really wasn't optional. If your TV, radio, or computer was on, it was playing the presidential address. Michelle looked and sounded calm, composed, and determined.

"Good Evening America. It's been a long day. I'm sure you're all wondering what happened today. I'll explain. Nine days ago, I pardoned Donald Trimp to keep Americans safe from a 'space weapon.' In the first seven days since Trimp's pardon, some 17,000 Americans were killed by gunfire. This is unacceptable, shameful, and embarrassing. Think about that for a minute. 17,000 people. A small percentage of our population hates each other so much, they're willing to murder a person over their political preferences, or the color of their skin, or their religious or sexual preferences. Therefore, to protect Americans from other Americans, I reluctantly signed an order proclaiming martial law. In the order were strict provisions curtailing the use of firearms. In a decent society, based on law and order, martial law and firearms restrictions would significantly slow the number of people dying by gunfire." She paused to shake her head sadly.

"It hurts me to say this. It's embarrassing. In the two days since we declared martial law, the killing increased. It's my job to keep Americans safe. In the two days since we declared martial law, a small percentage of Americans killed another 24,000 Americans. 41,000 Americans have died in the past nine days. 41,000.

"It's my job to keep Americans safe. So, this morning at 0400, we did just that. We adapted our new 'Space Force' technology to shut everything down. For now: don't worry about how we did that. Think instead about why we did that. Nothing mechanical or electrical would work today.

Guns, the internet, cell phones, TVs, radios. Cars. Guns. Electrical power. Did I mention guns?" She knew she had and smiled defiantly.

"Outbound flights were grounded. Incoming flights already airborne were redirected to Canada or Mexico. We were able to specifically keep the power on in key facilities such as hospitals, military bases, and distant warning sites.

"It's my job to keep Americans safe. And for the past few years, we have seemed intent on killing one another with guns. But the sheer level of violence has risen dramatically in these past nine days. So, this morning at 0400, we shut everything down. Our police forces, and our military personnel, with UN peacemakers' support, took some bold steps to make our country safer. From 0400 this morning until now, our security personnel arrested some 2.3 million persons breaking the firearms regulations specified in our proclamation of martial law. Our security personnel arrested those persons and seized almost 6 million firearms and many other weapons with minimum force.

"Those persons who were arrested are being held in stadiums, arenas, military bases, and corrections facilities. Those persons who willingly cooperated with our security forces will be processed for release as soon as possible. To keep Americans safe, we will need to maintain martial law over the next few days. We request that you see our security forces as a temporary measure, to keep us safe from ourselves.

I know that as a nation, we can rise above what we have recently become. This current state of affairs in our great nation is not who we are. We will emerge from this period of chaos into something better and brighter. People are scared right now. I get it. Trust me, I understand. My daughters and I have lived with that fear since 2008. Fear of haters. Fear of being shot." Michelle paused for a minute to let that sink in.

"But we have refused to let that fear change us or define who we are. In the coming days, our government will be discussing ways to end this cycle of hatred and violence. For now, I ask this. Be good to each other. Help each other. Be kind. Be decent and respectful. If we can do these small, simple acts, I believe that God will continue to bless America."

***

House of Representatives

A group of independent representatives had put forward a very controversial resolution, entitled: A Path to Peace. The longer they debated the issue, the more traction the resolution gained. People who initially hated the idea eventually came to love it and defend it. Trimp and his supporters loved it immediately. Most socialists, independents, or liberals saw sense in it. Younger people embraced the idea wholeheartedly. Older people and those with a traditional view of America liked it the least.

Other country's politicians hailed the plan as brilliant. "A Path to Peace will save millions of American lives," Germany's Angela Mercel said. "It will achieve peacefully what we have historically achieved by war."

Elijah loved it. "It's a brilliant resolution for America and Americans. Things change. Get over it. This resolution is merciful and smart. It allows an inevitable change to happen without bloodshed. It lets everyone maintain their respect and dignity. Honestly, the only other option at this point is a civil war. And what is the point of a civil war? For one side to defeat another by force and force the losing side to submit to the victor's will? Or for one side to fight the other until they are allowed to separate? This resolution will achieve that, peacefully, without all the horrible violence and expense of war. I've seen civil war through the eyes of a child. Don't put your kids through that. America, the whole world is hoping that you make the right decision."

After three days of debate and many amendments, annexes, and appendices, A Path to Peace was passed in the House of Representatives, 344 to 91. The resolution was sent to the Senate for sober second thought.

It was passed in two days, with 82 in favour and 18 opposing.

Trimp loved it.

***

CHAPTER 17.

The Gangrenous Leg

Ottawa

"We're speaking tonight with Benjamin Big Canoe, the Canadian Minister of Foreign Affairs. Mr. Big Canoe, our viewers in America might be surprised to learn that various Canadian provinces have discussed separation. What advice would you give to Americans right now who are concerned about the question of separation?"

"Well, first, Lester, I'd say that you are not alone. The United States is not the only country in the world having discussions about separation anxiety," Benjamin Big Canoe told Lester Bolt. "In Canada, some Quebecois have been thinking out loud about leaving our dominion and making a new country for sixty years. We've discussed granting nationhood to some of our First Nations bands. Albertans have discussed separation. Recently, Catalonia has been protesting for their independence from Spain.

Northern Ireland and Scotland are voting to leave the United Kingdom later this year. Look at the countries that have left Russia over the last 30 years: Moldova, Kyrgyzstan, Kazakhstan, Tajikistan, Uzbekistan, Armenia, Belarus, Ukraine, Lithuania, Latvia, Estonia… In 1993 Czechoslovakia peacefully dissolved and became the Czech Republic and Slovakia. By contrast, Yugoslavian factions were at war for 10 very violent years- from 1992 to 2002- before eventually accepting international arbiters' decisions on boundaries to become seven countries: Croatia, Bosnia-Herzegovina, Slovenia, Montenegro, Kosovo, North Macedonia, and Serbia. Think about that. Ten years of war, between factions who differed on religious practises and ethnic backgrounds."

"Regarding Quebec, how has the Canadian government managed to keep Quebec in Canada?"

"Great question. The answer is incredibly complex. In 1970, we had a national crisis when a terrorist group named Federation de Liberation du Quebec - the FLQ - kidnapped politicians and murdered one. It resulted in our government declaring the Emergency Measures Act. In 1995, Quebec held a referendum. The 'stay' side won, but the vote was incredibly close. 50.54 percent wanted to stay Canadian, and 49.46 percent wanted to leave. After the referendum, some of our citizens suggested that Canadians vote to kick Quebec out of Canada. Others accused the Canadian government of giving Quebec more money every time the topic of separation came up. That's partially true. The discussion of separation by Quebec has become quieter recently. Our First Nations people pointed out that if Quebec left Canada, 93 percent of the landmass would be given back to various indigenous bands under treaties signed with the Canadian government. We've been fortunate in Canada. The people who have discussed separatism have normally done so in a peaceful manner. We haven't been killing each other over political ideology or religious differences. It helps that we have very different gun laws than America."

"What are your thoughts on the 'Path to Peace' referendum that will allow Americans to vote on where they want to live?"

"I think it's brilliant. It means that Americans have accepted the cold hard fact that the left and right in America can no longer peacefully co-exist. 25 percent of your citizens want to have their ideology imposed on the other 75 percent. That 25 percent will not stop until they can live their lives as they choose. So you have 2 choices: a messy civil war or a peaceful solution. If you choose civil war, the side which is defeated will hate and resent the winners forever. Let the people choose. You can live in the United States, or live in Trimpistan."

"And what do you say to the Americans - on both sides of this argument - who don't want a divided America, who want our republic to remain the United States of America with all 50 states intact, who don't want to give up a square inch of territory?" Lester asked.

Benjamin smiled sadly. "Lester, I'd say that the time to salvage the United States of America as it was has passed. It's unfortunate, but nothing lasts forever. Honestly, take the emotion out of it, and look at the truth. The truth is that America's division is too deep to be repaired, and the hatred is too vicious and violent. If it helps, both sides could use a medical analogy here. If a doctor said you had a gangrenous leg that would kill you unless it was amputated, you would probably choose the amputation. You can still live with a new prosthetic leg. The people who choose to remain in the United States can consider those on the far right who choose Trimpistan as the gangrene. Conversely, the Trimp supporters can consider the crowd who choose not to follow Trimp as too liberal, too socialist, too... infected. The United States of America will still exist, just with less territory and fewer people. I'd say to those who choose to remain in the United States that you have a chance to improve your country, to move progressively in new directions. I'd tell those who choose to live in Trimpistan the same thing: this is your opportunity to live in a nation under laws that reflect your beliefs. I'd say that 'A Path to Peace' offers every person in your country a chance to choose to live in a country that suits you, without the messy, bloody, expensive pain of civil war. And finally, I wish everyone good luck. Good luck to those who choose to live in Trimpistan, and good luck to those who choose to remain in the United States."

"Thanks for this, Minister," Lester said, shaking Benjamin's hand.

***

Mar-a-Lago

Since OPERATION PEACEMAKER, the Niagara Regiment was busy tending to a multitude of angry prisoners. Those people who had voluntarily surrendered their firearms per the martial law directives had been processed and released. Their weapons were registered and locked in an armory. Those 2.3 million persons who had resisted arrest and refused to surrender their firearms were still incarcerated 12 days after OP PEACEMAKER.

As part of OP PEACEMAKER, the Oobima administration had temporarily seized some properties and assets it deemed as 'essential to the maintenance of peace.' The Trimp hotel at Mar-a-Lago met that 'essential' requirement. Like many hotels in the area, they had been filled with Trimp supporters who had flocked to that area to be near Trimp. They were holding prisoners who had been arrested during OP PEACEMAKER. Most of Trimp's domestic help at his multiple properties were undocumented workers from Mexico, Guatemala, and Nicaragua. The Oobima administration hired the staff there as essential workers at a government rate, which in most cases doubled or tripled their pay from what Trimp had been paying them. The properties and facilities temporarily used by the government were reimbursed at standard government rates if their business taxes were in order. In the case of Trimp Incorporated Properties, the IRS determined that Trimp owed hundreds of millions in back taxes and prepared legal documents to seize the properties permanently as payment of said taxes.

The 'Southern White House' itself was being used as a command post for that part of Florida. Various directors from the US Armed Forces, Homeland Security, State Police, and the UN peacekeepers coordinated regional efforts from the 'Big House' at Mar-a-Lago.

Trimp was issued a room on the second floor of his hotel with 3 Trimpanzee men who adored him. Spending personal time with Trimp was the greatest moment of their lives. It was the lowest point in Trimp's. Ted was a Vietnam vet with some anger management and incontinence issues. Frank was a mechanic in his early forties who had drifted from town to town across the rust belt. Bob was a soybean farmer from Kansas who had lost his fourth-generation farm to Trimp's disastrous economic management of tariffs.

The room was a standard budget with two double beds. The room had a view overlooking the parking lot, the dumpsters, and the kitchen's delivery ramp. The internet and cable to the rooms were switched off. The prisoner's cell phones had been confiscated. Ted, Frank, and Bob thought the room was wonderful and luxurious. They were proud to have been arrested as part of Trimp's self-proclaimed 'Freedom Fighters.'

Fabiola, Lumpy, T-Bone, and many other Canadian peacekeepers started their day with a mandatory workout from 0600 to 0630. Their breakfast at the mess hall was from 0700 to 0730. At 0740, they were driven in APC's and buses to start their day at Mar-a-Lago. Some of the peacekeepers patrolled the 'area of separation' set up to keep folks clear of the detainee facilities. The soldiers served the detainees breakfast in their rooms between 0800 and 0830. Lunch was from 1230 to 1300. Supper was served from 1730-1800. The meals met the minimum nutritional guidelines and cost standards established for Florida State prisons. The Oobima administration had re-assigned supervisors from various prisons in Florida to ensure that the detainees were cared for following state standards. The detainees were allowed a half-hour walk each day around the hotel parking lot, which doubled as the exercise yard.

When they weren't delivering meals, the peacekeepers helped the hotel staff with meal preparation: peeling potatoes, carrots, and onions, dicing and slicing vegetables for salads, washing pots, and so on. They did yard maintenance and cleaned the pool. They worked out in the gym in shifts.

Fabiola found that she enjoyed the meal delivery part of the job the most. Three times a day, Fabiola, Lumpy, and an American military policewoman - July Jefferson - delivered meals to 100 people in 25 rooms. Lumpy passed out the trays, and Fabiola and July stood by with tasers if anyone got unruly.

Unruly, like the girls in room 625. When they opened the door, Fabiola saw the angry, bleached blonde "Proud Racist Bitch' lady that she had tasered during OP PEACEMAKER.

"Well, if it isn't the little Mexican bitch who tasered me," she began, looking angrily between Fabiola and Sergeant Jefferson. Her eyes rested on Jefferson's nametag. "Jefferson, I want to complain to a WHITE American officer. Last week, I was trying to surrender peacefully, and this wetback bitch tasered me!" she said haughtily. Her roommates were all clamoring for Sergeant Jefferson to "do something." You could smell the hate in the room. The bleached blondes were angrier than wet hens. They were also starting to get a little too close.

"Well, first, all four of you 'ladies' step back while I speak with this soldier," Sgt Jefferson said in a threatening voice while waving her taser. "Is this true, Private Gonzalez?" Sgt Jefferson asked.

"It's true," Fabiola said, blushing. "We were handcuffing the hotel staff who had surrendered when this lady came out. She said, 'I surrender, but I will NOT be handcuffed to a Nigger, a Chink or a Mexican.'"

"She's lying," shrieked the blonde lady. "You can't believe a lying Mexican over an American citi...aieeeeee!"

She didn't get to finish her rebuttal. Sergeant Jefferson zapped her with the taser. "Prisoner, you need to stop referring to this soldier as a Mexican. Private Gonzalez, show this prisoner the flag on your shoulders." Fabiola turned sideways as directed. The blonde lady was on the floor, eyes full of hate. "You see, that is a Canadian flag," Jefferson continued. "So you calling her a Mexican is just stupid. She is not from Mexico, by the way. From this point forward, you will refer to her as Private Gonzalez. Lemme hear you say it. Say her name," Sgt Jefferson insisted angrily, waving the taser again.

"Private Gonzalez," the woman said quietly. She sat up slowly.

"Very good. Enjoy your rice and beans, ladies. Just put those trays on the table, and we'll let our guests enjoy their meal," Jefferson said to Lumpy and Fabiola. They closed the door.

"Don't be afraid of these crackers," Sergeant Jefferson told Fabiola, who nodded her head but still looked puzzled.

Lumpy had to explain what a 'cracker' was to Fabiola.

"Ahhh, like that lady? Crackers just hate everybody who's not white and from the southern states?"

Lumpy nodded. "Exactly."

"OK. Now I get it." Fabiola noticed that most of the detainees really resented having someone with a thick Latina accent or a black woman like July in a position of authority over them. That made her play up her accent even more. *Pendejos, I'll show you some Latina...*

"Damn girl, you're getting good at this detainee thing," July laughed at the end of their shift. "Feel's good seeing privileged criminals held accountable, yes?"

Fabiola smiled weakly and nodded. *Is it that obvious?* she wondered. *Father Jakub will know what to do...*

"Father, forgive me, for I have sinned. Please help me repent and do no further harm."

"What was the nature of your sin?" Padre Jakub asked. He'd been Fabiola's parish priest for several years since her family had arrived in Niagara Falls. Her family was very devout.

"I'm not a mean person padre, but lately, I enjoy seeing mean people getting punished for their, uhh ...meanness," she told Father Jakub in confession. "Is that a sin?"

"Great question. It's human nature for sure. When we live within established rules and laws, it's normal for us to want lawbreakers punished. Without punishment or consequences, no one would follow society's rules or government laws. You aren't directly punishing these people. They are being detained because they broke the laws of their country. You're not punishing them: you're helping them, bringing them meals."

"I just don't wanna become mean and angry like these people. The people locked up here are not very nice. They say mean things, call me a stupid Mexican bitch..." Fabiola sniffed. She told Father Jakub about the angry blonde lady.

"It's a stressful time for everyone," Father Jakub said softly. "The people being detained are feeling embarrassed and angry. All you can do is try to understand how they are feeling. Don't let their anger and hate hurt you. Try to deflect their hate with kindness. Be pleasant and polite, but remember, most importantly, to keep yourself safe. Keep your guard up; stay alert. You've done nothing wrong. I think Jesus himself would have tasered the blonde bitch. Go with God's blessing."

Fabiola seemed relieved. "Thank you, padre."

Forgive me, father, Jakub silently prayed. *Am I a bad priest?*

***

CHAPTER 18.

By The Sweat Of His Brow

St Jacobs Ontario

"Good morning, brothers and sisters," a young Amish man began quietly. He and all the Amish men were dressed all in black, with a dark blue shirt. "My name is Elmo Stoll. I'm an elder here in our Amish community in St Jacob's. Welcome to our first community workshop on sustainable farming. Welcome to a ...simpler lifestyle. We kindly ask that you respect our customs and traditions during your stay here as per the joining instructions we mailed you. Do not photograph our people, do not introduce social media to our people, and refrain from foul language, smoking, drugs, and alcohol..."

The Amish community had approached the workshop idea cautiously. As an old farmer, Charley Shackleton, the Canadian Minister of Agriculture, had long admired the Amish methods. Charley and his Simpleton hippy wife Dorothy had encouraged the Amish to share their knowledge with the world. They did not use tractors, trucks, or any motorized equipment. When asked why, the Amish would shyly reply, "Our Bible tells us that *'Man should earn his bread by the sweat of his brow, until we return to the fertile soil, since from it we were taken; we are soil, to the soil we shall return.'*" Regardless of where the Amish drew their inspiration from, atheists, agnostics, and people of all religious persuasions agreed that the Amish farming practises were sensible, sustainable, environmentally friendly, healthy, and practical. They did not use pesticides, insecticides, or chemical fertilizers. Many of their grain and vegetable crops and livestock breeds were old-world stock passed down through generations back to the 1800s. They always kept a percentage of their harvest to dry as seed for future crops. They had never planted genetically modified crops or injected their animals with drugs.

A month before hosting their own workshop, Elmo, his son Jeremiah and two other young Amish men had travelled by train to SimpleTown, British Columbia. SimpleTown was a commune started by Less Izmore in the late 1980s. The members of the commune had studied, and mimicked Amish agricultural practises and construction techniques for years. Elmo, Ishamel, and Gideon were very impressed with what the Simpletons had created. A few of the Simpletons that created the original commune were still living there, but many more had moved on. Some had started other simple 'back to the land' communes all over the world. Less Izmore, a former bank executive and the founding father of SimpleTown, was serving as Canada's Finance Minister. KT Burfitt was SimpleTown's newest elder. KT was a former journalist for the BC Sun. She visited the commune to write a story on the 'crazy hippies' and fell in love with the Simpleton way of life. While in SimpleTown, she had gained a daughter, Susanna.

SimpleTown was an excellent choice to slowly introduce Amish people to a world other than their own. The community was quiet, respectful, and loving. For their part, Elmo, Jeremiah, Ishmael, and Gideon had only ever been to the small town of St Jacobs to sell produce from their farm. So meeting the diverse crowd in SimpleTown was very educational for the Amish men. There were students from India, Africa, Vietnam, Syria, Mexico, the USA, Israel, Ecuador, Russia, China, Iceland, and Ireland. Many of the students were already farmers. They were all keen on learning new (often meaning old or resurrected) practises that could help them farm in a sustainable, planet-friendly way.

SimpleTown was about as Amish as a community could be in many ways. Both communities had their own schools and worked together to ensure that everyone in the community had a similar lifestyle. There were no rich or poor members in either community. The only difference between the two was their beliefs and customs based on religion. The Amish were devout Christians; all their customs, beliefs, and traditions were based on Biblical teachings. The Simpletons had no preferred religious beliefs, but everybody there followed the Golden Rule.

Elmo Stoll had married his childhood sweetheart Ruth when they were both 15 years old. Ruth died in childbirth ten months after they were married. Their son Jeremiah survived, and the local women in the Amish community helped Elmo raise him. Elmo was heartbroken and never really got over losing Ruth. Although there were other eligible young Amish ladies his friends suggested as suitable wives, Elmo had remained a widower for the eight years following Ruth's death.

During his visit to SimpleTown, KT, Elmo, Jeremiah, and Susanna became good friends. It was pretty obvious. "You are both elders in your community and single parents," Ishmael teased a blushing Elmo.

KT heard the same thing from Simpletons about her 'Amish boyfriend.' She laughed it off. "I'm not gonna become an Amish woman, you goofballs," she told her friends through a big lungful of BC bud. "He's an adorably sweet person, but I don't think Elmo Stoll is going to renounce his beliefs and community to chase some crazy hippy girl around."

Despite her assurances that nothing could be made of their friendship, no one in SimpleTown was surprised when KT and Susanna booked tickets to attend the Amish workshop in St Jacobs.

***

Washington DC

After a long debate in the US Senate, the 'Path to Peace' resolution had carried with 82 Senators in favor and 12 opposed. President Oobima and Vice President John-Stone explained what was at stake and how the vote would work.

It was similar to the vote that citizens in Scotland, Catalonia, and Quebec had recently done. "Americans have two choices in this election," 'The Stone' said. "You can choose to 'Stay' and remain as a citizen of the United States. If that's the case, you don't need to do anything. We will assume that you wish to remain a citizen of these United States unless you vote to 'Leave.' If you vote to 'Leave' the United States and become a citizen of Trimpistan, there will be two ways to register a 'Leave' vote. The first option will be online at www.usgovernment.leave. The second option will be by mail: all United States Post Offices will have ballots that are postage paid.

"Where will Trimpistan be located is what everybody wants to know. It's a great question. Honestly, we won't know the answer until we've tallied the votes. As we have explained, Trimpistan will be allocated 1 square mile of territory for every 100 citizens. That is the current population density of the United States. There are, on average, 100 Americans on each square mile of territory."

A map of the continental United States appeared behind the vice president. 'The Stone' kept speaking while the map highlighted some states for viewers. "For example, if four million Americans vote to become citizens of Trimpistan, that new country will be given forty thousand square miles of territory - which is roughly the size of Kentucky. If eight million people vote to 'Leave,' the corresponding territory would be the size of Kansas." The vice president handed off to Michelle Oobima. "Madam President."

Michelle picked up where the vice president left off. "Our elected officials in Congress and the Senate agreed on the following principles in regards to allocation of territory.

1. The United States Congress will determine which land will be allocated to Trimpistan. Consideration will be given to regional voter density to minimize the need for people to relocate.
2. Trimpistan will be allocated a blend of rural, suburban, and urban territory.
3. Those citizens who choose to become citizens of Trimpistan must move into their new nation

within six months of Trimpistan's formation. Those citizens will surrender their United States passport and citizenship. Citizens of Trimpistan will have two years after the country's formation to sell their property in the United States. After the two years have passed, the property will become an asset of the United States.

4. Citizens of the United States who own property in the territory designated for Trimpistan will be given moving allowances to relocate in the United States. Citizens of the United States will have two years after Trimpistan's formation to sell their property in Trimpistan. After the two years have passed, the property will become an asset of Trimpistan. The United States will reimburse Americans for any losses incurred in the sale of property and businesses. The United States government will then bill the government of Trimpistan that amount.

5. The United States Government retains the right to remove federal and state facilities, equipment, and assets for a period of up to five years after Trimpistan's formation. The United States government reserves the right to restrict access of Trimpistan citizens into the United States. The government of Trimpistan reserves the right to restrict access of American citizens into Trimpistan.

Michelle paused. "As you might expect, the points I've mentioned are the highlights, not an exhaustive list. The entire agreement can be seen at www.pathtopeace.gov. I encourage everyone to read the agreement before you decide. I'll be meeting with Trimp to discuss the agreement in several days. Our executive team from this administration will meet with Trimp's team to further refine these details. We will set a date for voting and discuss the way ahead. I encourage people to keep an open mind about this peace process. Whether you have been a Trimp supporter since 2016, or if you have recently become a Trimp supporter, I encourage you to continue to support Donald Trimp. It's in the interest of everyone that you make the right choice here. Please don't stay in America and work against us if you are a Trimp supporter. If you believe that Donald Trimp will build a nation that supports your beliefs, we encourage you to choose to 'Leave' America and become a citizen of Trimpistan."

***

Mar-a-Lago

The Oobima - Trimp summit was quite a spectacle. The summit took place at Mar-a-Lago. The meeting between President Oobima and Donald Trimp lasted two minutes. Just long enough to show footage of the two seated across a desk from each other with a trusted team of advisors. Trimp's team included Donald Jr, Eric, Jared Kirschner, Roger Stones, Paul Manafart, Stephen Miller, Mike Pens, and Mitch MacDonald. As a gesture of good faith, President Oobima had also arranged for the Chinese to release Ivanka. As she entered the room, most viewers could see that incarceration had not been kind to her.

Trimp was pale, sullen, sweaty, and morose. He brightened up considerably when Ivanka was presented. Still, it was obvious that both of them needed a few weeks in tanning booths and with makeup professionals to return to their former appearances.

President Oobima gave Trimp and his associates access to the internet and returned their cellphones. Trimp needed a headquarters or home base, so he agreed to rent Mar-a-Lago from the US government for $45,000.00 per day. His first act with his cellphone was to appeal to Trimp supporters to donate to the Trimpistan foundation in support of Trimplican relocation and support programs. Trimp critics pointed out that any money given to Trimp would be spent on a Trimp first, and all others last.

After eight days of meetings between the delegates from the United States and Trimpistan, President Oobima and President Trimp signed the historical document outlining the path to peace through separation. The vote was arranged for the last week of July. Following the vote, the United States Congress would determine Trimpistan's location.

Ivanka and Jared started a Trimpistan savings bond campaign. Investors were guaranteed a 5% annual rate of return. "The savings bonds will be used to purchase advertising for the 'Leave' campaign, and a small salary for Trimpistan's executive team," Ivanka explained in the first ad. Trimp himself generously agreed to donate his new presidential salary from Trimpistan to orphaned children of Trimpanzees killed during the recent civil unrest.

"Donald Trimp is the world's most generous man," Hanratty gushed.

Tommi Loren agreed. "Sean, Donald Trimp will build the new Utopia. I can't wait to live in Trimpistan. I mean, look at this new Constitution of Trimpistan! Low taxes, freedom, small government, and no socialism. What an exciting time to be alive. If you love freedom, you'll want to live in Trimpistan. It'll be like America was back when America was great."

The Trimpistan campaign generated an astonishing amount of money within several days. The advertisements on TV and FaceBook to 'Leave' the United States and join Trimpistan were compelling. For loyal Trimp supporters. The ads were attack pieces against anyone wanting to remain in *"A ruined shell of America filled with socialists, leftists, communists, homosexuals, atheists, snowflakes and coastal elites."* A FOX News poll suggested that 150 million American's were planning to 'Leave.'

***

CHAPTER 19.
Meat Shields

Fort McMurray, Alberta

Elijah studied the project numbers on the flight out to refresh his memory. The prime minister was flying in the latest Royal Canadian Air Force Otter. The plane was made of carbon fibre and powered by an electric motor and batteries. It was a two-hour visit to officially open a large renewable power project, tour the facility, and do a grip and grin with the workers. The Otter's pilot flew in over a ten-kilometre stretch of wind turbines and quietly brought the Otter down in a field beside the project offices and maintenance buildings.

"Sir, our intelligence on the ground suggests a crowd of about 10,000 people. There are 7500 friendlies and 2500 protestors," his RCMP security chief advised. Lateef had been head of security to the last two Canadian prime ministers.

Elijah smiled. "It wouldn't be a democracy if we all agreed on everything all the time."

"Let us meat shields get in place before you exit, Sir," Lateef reminded Elijah. "And we'll go straight to the dais, please. It should take us 15 seconds."

"Wait. What? Who calls you 'meat shields'? That's very disrespectful."

"We call ourselves that, Sir. It's black humour for cops. It would only be disrespectful if someone else called us that."

Lateef and his detail deplaned first, then Lateef nodded at the prime minister. Elijah was a security nightmare. He liked people too much and would often veer out of his security pocket to shake hands or talk to people. This occasion was no different. After two minutes of high fiving the crowd, they made it to the dais. Elijah bounded to the podium. A large cheer, made louder by boos from 25 percent of the crowd, greeted him.

"This is a great day for Alberta, and a great day for Canada," he began. "First thing: how about a big round of applause for all the workers who made this dream a reality." It was a safe ask. About 7500 of the workers were in the crowd.

"Facts and figures are fun," Elijah continued. "This turbine project will add 850 megawatts of power to southern Alberta's electrical output annually. The frames and blades for the turbines were made from Athabasca tar sand carbon fibre." Big cheer from the carbon fibre crowd. "This project proved that we can use our tar sand for more than just fuel." Some applause, some boos. "The carbon dioxide offset for that much wind-generated power is 4 million metric tonnes, or the equivalent of taking a million cars off the road." Boos from the anti windmill crowd.

Elijah was well known for going off-script.

"OK. I gotta know. Who boos an economic and environmental win like this? Put your hands up."

The 2500 anti-wind pro-oil protestors cheered lustily and hoisted signs while the other 7500 people booed them. Their signs were pretty good.

'Windmills Cause Cancer'

'Canada Runs On Alberta Oil'

'God Gave us Oil, Not Windmills.' And so on.

Elijah raised his hands and asked for quiet. "Listen, please. I want to address those of you who don't like this project." The crowd settled a bit. "Now I understand that you're not happy with this new direction. We've calmly and rationally outlined why it makes good environmental and economic sense to use our tar sand to make carbon fibre rather than burn it as fuel. And we've done our best to ensure that we retain and retrain workers from the oil patch to work in this new field. There is no economic or environmental sense in using our tar sand as fuel beyond 2040. We've implemented a plan to gradually reduce oil production in Alberta and generate power from renewable sources." *Boos.*

"Is there anybody here who used to be a coal miner?" Elijah asked.

About 500 hands went up, mostly from older men.

Elijah went to the front of the stage and pointed to the man closest. Lateef and the security detail looked nervously in the crowd. "Sir, what happened to your town when the coal mines started closing?" He hopped off the stage and handed the man a microphone. A young lady from tech support brought Elijah another mike. "And tell us your name," Elijah added.

"I'm Albert MacInnis - *cheers* - My home town? New Waterford's pretty much a ghost town now," the old miner said. "When the mines closed, real estate crumbled, stores started closing, and the young people all left. We tried to hang on, but there weren't any jobs. I left Cape Breton and hitch-hiked out here in 81 and been here ever since. I guess I call Fort Mac home now," he said to more cheers.

"So as a former coal miner, how did you feel about oil and gas putting coal out of business?"

"Well...most of us was pissed off that we had to move to find work. Some of the older people back home who wouldn't or couldn't move just stayed there and died angry." There were murmurs of agreement from the other old miners. "And now I think most of us are angry at these green people who say that oil is bad and dirty, and we all need to stop using it right away. We've got some of the best safety standards and the best oil field workers in the world right here. I'm proud to work here in Fort McMurray." The folks around him applauded. "I guess most of us just don't wanna feel guilty about the work we've been doing. It's good honest work. We've done our best to do it cleanly and safely. In the last few years, oilmen have been painted as environmental criminals by people who turn around and use our Alberta oil to heat their homes, make electricity, and fuel their cars and planes. We're not bad people, but folks have sure tried to shame us just for earning an honest living." A big cheer went up for Albert. He said what they were all thinking.

"I get it. I'm sorry you've been made to feel that way. As a leader of a green revolution, I know we've been, um... enthusiastic about transitioning to renewable energy. We have sometimes painted the oil industry in a bad light in our enthusiasm to convert people to green energy. I don't think it was ever our intent to attack the people who work in that industry. But it sounds like that has happened, so I'll apologise personally to all of you here today," Elijah said. He shook Albert's hand, then gave him a big hug. The crowd liked that.

"Our goal has always been a gradual, safe, environmentally friendly, economically viable transition from oil and gas to renewable energy. Now here it is 40 years after oil replaced coal, and a new, better, smarter, cheaper, cleaner technology is going to replace gas and oil." The carbon fibre crowd cheered. "Look, I know it's hard to change careers. I know you're all proud to work in the oil patch here, and you should be proud. *Cheers.* Alberta oil, dug out by all you folks, has been Canada's economic engine for the past 50 years, and you should all be proud of that." *Louder cheers.* Elijah patted Albert on the shoulder and took the mike back, and hopped on the stage again. "Albert, we're not asking you and your coworkers to move again," Elijah said quietly.

"We're just doing something different with the oil. Instead of burning it, we can use it to make carbon fibre. It'll make us all more money this way. Alberta tar sands are still a great resource and a tremendous blessing. We just want to use it in a new way, a more sustainable way. I hope you can all come to terms with this change. No one needs to move. No one is losing their job. In fact, the transition to renewable energy, boosted by carbon fibre revenue, will be a job creator." Elijah went quiet. After a few seconds, Albert MacInnis began to applaud. The applause was picked up by his fellow former coal miners and wind turbine protestors and then grew to a roar.

Albert and Elijah's discussion was the lead story on Canadian news. Alberta carbon fibre got a huge boost as the story went global.

Meanwhile, Elijah and his team were heading north to visit a huge mine opened by the Dogrib band at Great Slave Lake. The transition from oil to renewable energy would require new resources to store the power created. The mine at Great Slave Lake had tremendous deposits of copper, molybdenum, zinc, nickel, and lead. To be truly 'green,' those minerals had to be extracted safely, with the smallest possible environmental impact.

***

Washington DC

Madam President, is your administration going to run ads encouraging citizens to 'Stay' in the United States?"

"No."

"Have you seen the advertisements encouraging Americans to 'Leave' the United States and become citizens of Trimpistan?"

President Oobima smiled. "I have seen the ads for Trimpistan. I just don't feel we need to sell anyone on what a great country America is. I don't want to discourage anyone from joining Donald Trimp in Trimpistan. As our future new neighbors, Americans should pray that Trimpistan is prosperous and successful. We passed a resolution to allow for a peaceful separation between ideologies that couldn't agree. This peaceful path to separation is much better than the civil war which seemed inevitable just weeks ago. I've said many times: it's in the best interest of the United States and Trimpistan that people choose wisely. If Trimpistan sounds like a place where you believe that you'll be happier than you have been in America, you should vote to 'Leave.'"

***

CHAPTER 20.

Are You Staying? Or Leaving?

Throughout July of 2021, the advertisements urging Americans to 'Leave' America and become Trimplicans was relentless. The ads became increasingly negative, attacking America as a failed state and promising a glorious future for Trimpistan. Many advertisements were multiplied exponentially on social media, which spawned vicious, hateful arguments between 'Stayers' and 'Leavers.' President Oobima and her administration did not respond to the attack ads. Her message to Americans remained simple and consistent. "I encourage all Americans to choose wisely in the upcoming election. I'm not going to try and convince you to remain in the United States. If you believe that Trimpistan has a bright future, you should vote to 'Leave.' If you admire and respect Donald Trimp and believe that he will lead Trimpistan to greatness, you should vote to 'Leave.'"

Trimp's administration courted businesses aggressively. They promised generous relocation packages and low corporate tax rates for owners. Trimps remarkable acumen as a titan of business was flaunted. Ivanka was given credit for the creation of more than 15 million jobs in 2018. The 'My Pillow' guy endorsed Trimp and promised he'd relocate to Trimpistan.

Evangelical support was also strong. Frankland Graham, Paulette White, and many of their kind preached that Trimpistan was God's new chosen land. During July, most of their sermons were fire and brimstone for those choosing to remain in Sodom and Gomorrah. Michelle Oobima was referred to as 'that Muslim woman,' 'that godless woman,' or 'that godless Muslim woman.'

When voting began on 18 July, erratic and erroneous claims were rampant. Alex Janes claimed that 137 million Americans voted to 'Leave' on the first day. FOX News ran similar stories, with multiple witnesses who couldn't wait to start a new life in Trimpistan.

President Oobima's administration reminded journalists that the election results were being closely guarded until 31 July. No numbers would be released before that date. July 2021 was breaking records for heat across North America and Europe. In America, the days dragged slowly towards the end of the month.

***

Mar-a-Lago

The Niagara peacekeepers had settled into a routine. The troops worked 12-hour shifts patrolling the Area of Separation. They had formed bonds of brotherhood with their American counterparts in uniform.

Sergeant Major Lee knew that 'routine' was a dangerous thing for peacekeepers. She continued to train the troops at a demanding pace. She sprang surprise exercises on them at random unexpected hours. "Stay alert, stay alive!" was her consistent message to the troops each morning at 0700. She continually reminded them of the danger of becoming complacent. "There are still many people here who resent our presence, who resent that we took their firearms. Given a chance, they will harm or kill you. Do not let your guard down."

On 30 July, the Niagara Regiment was given a cruel reminder of the need to stay alert.

CANADIAN FORCES SIGNIFICANT INCIDENT MESSAGE: 1205Z30 JULY 2021.

1. FOUR CANADIAN PEACEKEEPERS AND THREE AMERICAN FORCES PERSONNEL WERE KILLED BY AN IMPROVISED EXPLOSIVE DEVICE IN THE TRIMP HOTEL AT MAR-A-LAGO.

2. NAMES ARE BEING WITHHELD AT THIS TIME IN ORDER TO NOTIFY NEXT OF KIN.

3. THIRTY TWO CANADIAN PEACEKEEPERS ARE REPORTED AS INJURED, ELEVEN CRITICALLY. SEVENTEEN AMERICAN FORCES PERSONNEL ARE INJURED, NINE CRITICALLY.

4. INVESTIGATION IS ONGOING. EARLY REPORTS INDICATE THAT THE BOMB MAKER WAS A FORMER MEMBER OF US ARMY.

END MESSAGE.

Padre Jakub and 23 soldiers from the Niagara Regiment had just returned home for ten days of leave. He had been eager to return to his parishioners and was justifiably proud of the growth his church was experiencing. He took the opportunity to speak at Mass and officiated a baptism. He was greeting parishioners as they left his church when the Regiment's Commanding Officer and Chief of Staff pulled up in a black staff car. Both officers stepped out of the car in full dress uniform and waited quietly while Jakub shook the last few hands.

Father Jakub's heart sunk when he noticed they were wearing black armbands over their uniform. "Father Antonio, I'll need you to lock up," he said quietly to his understudy. "I'll call you later."

"I'm afraid we have terrible news," the CO began. "We need to act quickly. I'll brief you in the car." As the

Chief of Staff drove, Colonel Morrison explained the task ahead. "Here are the names of the soldiers we lost and the addresses we need to visit. We need to inform their families before the story breaks in the press." The first address was Gramma Hannah's boarding house, where Father Jakub and three Niagaras were staying while they were home on leave.

"Hannah and Rosa just left the church five minutes ago," Father Jakub whispered to himself.

Gramma Hannah was Lumpy's grandmother, but everybody in Ste Catherines called her Gramma. She ran a boarding house in a huge funky old Victorian home and rented dorm-style rooms to twenty people. When the Gonzalez family first came to Canada, they had stayed with her until they moved to their farm. Fabiola's grandmother Rosa stayed on at Hannah's to help her run the boarding house.

Hannah and Rosa both came to the door. "Father Jakub, you know you don't need to knock," she chided him in Polish. "You live here. Just come in." She then noticed the other two officers. "Why are you crying, Father?" she asked in English.

"Hannah, we need to speak privately with you and Rosa."

Both ladies began to cry softly as Jakub led the way to a small library. "Please, sit," Jakub implored. Both ladies shook their heads.

"Just tell us, Father," Rosa whispered.

"I'm afraid we have bad news for both of you," he began. "T-Bone was killed early this morning in an explosion, and both Lumpy and Fabiola are injured." The women sobbed quietly as Padre Jakub continued. "Hannah, you know T-Bone's family history. He considered you as his Gramma and listed you as his legal next of kin when he joined the army. Do you know where his parents are?"

Hannah nodded quietly. "I have his mother's phone number if it still works. T-Bone never talked about his father. He might be dead. Or, at least, T-Bone used to say, '*his father was dead to him.*' Oh, this is so terrible..." Hannah's voice trailed off.

***

The vote to "Leave" concluded on the last day of July in 2021. The polling places had been quiet and peaceful in comparison to the 2020 election. Many of the Trimpanzees were offended that America had not worked harder to encourage them to 'Stay' in America. Other 'Leavers' were disappointed that there were no libtard snowflakes protesting at the polling places they could assault, intimidate or harass.

The Canadian peacekeepers and American security personnel who monitored the polling places were pleasantly surprised at how peaceful the 'Stay or Leave' vote was.

On 31 July, President Oobima addressed her nation. "My fellow Americans. Tonight at 8 PM, voting to 'Leave' America concluded. I want to thank the volunteers who worked in all the polling places. I also want to thank our American military personnel, the UN peacekeepers, and our own police forces who worked together to ensure peace and order were maintained during this vote. I understand this is an emotional issue for all of us. Although we are still receiving some numbers from our polling places, I will tell you what I know.

"At this point, approximately 37,365,000 Americans have voted that they will renounce their American citizenship and become citizens of Trimpistan. We anticipate that the number may go as high as 38 million once all the votes have been tallied.

"The population density of the United States is 100 persons per square mile. As agreed in the Path to Peace accord, Trimpistan will be awarded one square mile for every hundred citizens who chose to leave. During the accord discussions, delegates from the United States and Trimpistan agreed that the boundaries of Trimpistan would be drawn by a committee of 50 congressmen and congresswomen. Based on 37 to 38 million voters who chose to leave America, that committee will choose a geographic area of 370,000 to 380,000 square miles. Our committee will meet tomorrow morning to begin those discussions. We hope that the committee will present their decision in several weeks. In the meantime, I ask everyone, Americans, and citizens of Trimpistan, to remain calm and be kind to each other. Good night, and may God richly bless both our nations as we move forward on the Path to Peace."

On completion of the presidential address, the talking heads and pundits on every network began to speculate about what Trimpistan's border could or should be.

"Put Trimpistan in Alaska,' said a far-left news panelist. "Seriously. There's plenty of room, and the Trimpistanis can build their Utopia there. No border issues with other American states, lots of resources. It's the easiest solution. Alaska had the third-highest percentage of 'Leave' voters per capita. America owes the Trimpistanis nothing. They chose to leave. Boom. Done."

Trimp's new citizens referred to themselves as Trimplicans. "It sounds like American, but better," Trimp had said on Parler. He'd been kicked off Twitter for repeated ethics violations and hate speech. Everyone else referred to them as Trimpistanis, Trimpanzees, MAGAts, or worse.

Meanwhile, on Fox News, the Trimp children insisted that they should be on the boundary committee. "Trimplicans must have a say in determining our boundaries," Ivanka said. "We demand that Trimpistan must include all of Florida at minimum, and the

Carolinas, and the nice, non-immigranty part of New York City because Daddy has so many golf courses and hotels in those places..."

Sean Hanratty didn't have the heart to remind Ivanka that all of Trimp's properties had been seized by the United States government as reparation for hundreds of millions of dollars in back taxes.

****

The Trimpistan boundary committee took its task seriously. It was being chaired by Alexandria Occasional-Cortez -AOC - a young IPP Congresswoman from New York. The 50 congressmen and women had been selected by President Oobima, with one representative from each state.

There were five Republicans who had been selected specifically because they voted to 'Leave.' "I don't want the citizens of Trimpistan to say that they had no representation on this committee," President Oobima said.

The rest of the committee was composed of eleven Democrats and thirty-four Independent Representatives, which was the equivalent proportional representation of each party in congress.

AOC called the meeting to order with a gavel. "Welcome to the Trimpistan boundary committee meeting. Seven days ago, each of us received their nominations to this committee and copies of the Path to Peace agreement."

To say that AOC was a polarising figure would be an understatement. The young IPP congresswoman was loathed by far-right conservatives and beloved anyone who leaned left. There was no middle ground. Even those who hated her the most grudgingly admitted she was always well organised and came to every discussion armed with real proven facts, figures, and documents. Which was another reason they hated her.

"I bring the committee member's attention to article three, sub-section seven, which defines this committee's task. As of this morning, the final number of citizens who voted to 'Leave' America and live in Trimpistan is 37,859,642. Another way to consider these numbers is as a percentage of our population. By this metric, 8.94 percent of American citizens have elected to rescind their American citizenship to become citizens of Trimpistan. That number includes some seven million children under the age of majority who sadly have no choice in this matter. Therefore, as per Sub-Section Seven, our job is to outline a geographic area measuring 378, 596.5 square miles of territory or 8.94% of US territory that can be ceded from the United States to Trimpistan.

"I remind our committee members to focus on a solution that ensures Trimpistan has a reasonable mix of cities, suburbs, arable land, and wilderness. Remember, we want Trimpistan to be successful. The geographical area we select may include coastline, lakes, and waterways. The proposed area should consider state voting preferences to ensure the least disruption to American citizens by citizens of Trimpistan. For example, only 1.3 percent of California's citizens voted to 'Leave.' By contrast, 41 percent of Wyoming's citizens voted to become citizens of Trimpistan. At this point, the floor is open for suggestions."

A Republican congressman from Iowa was on already on his feet." Yes, Congressman Jones. The chair recognises the congressman from Idaho."

"Thank you, Ma'am. As one of five members of this committee who was smart enough to vote to 'Leave,' I have a proposal." The House of Representatives groaned or booed their displeasure at the 'Leaver's' comment. They found themselves looking at a map on a big screen. The map included all of Florida, clear over to Arizona, up to Idaho, along the Canadian border to Ohio, and back down the coast from South Carolina to Virginia. The territory on the map identified as 'People's Republic of Trimpistan' was highlighted in orange. The House of Representatives looked at the map in a mix of shock and horror and then began to laugh.

Bang! Bang! Bang! "Order, please." The House pulled themselves together, with some representatives clearly stifling the urge to laugh. "Congressman Jones: how many square miles of territory are included in your proposal?" AOC asked.

"Uhhhh, honestly, I'm not sure. I prepared this map a month ago when President Trimp suggested that he anticipated Trimpistan's population would exceed 200 million citizens."

"Madam Chair, the congressman's proposed territory covers 77.4 % of the landmass of the contiguous 48 states," a staff geographer from the Department of Interior interjected.

"Thank you for that information. Congressman Jones, your proposal does not meet the parameters required of this committee. Please be seated. Yes, Congressman LaPlante. The chair recognises the representative from Vermont."

"Thank you, Madam Chair. My proposal is quite simple and practical. I propose that we cede Trimpistanis and Trimp 500,000 square miles of territory in Alaska." The territory on the congressman's map was outlined in the shape of Trimp's head from a side perspective and colored orange. Again, the house broke out in guffaws and laughter. "The reason for the extra territory is to make up for the difficult climate that Alaska has. Let's be honest here. None of our American citizens want to live near the border of Trimpistan. If the goal of our democracy is to do the most good for the majority of our American citizens, this proposal is perfect. The territory I'm proposing is resource-rich and offers Trimpistanis wide-open spaces to drive their trucks, hunt, and fish. This proposal requires the least amount of Americans to leave territory ceded to Trimpistan. This proposal means only patriotic Alaskans and our good Canadian friends would have to share borders with Trimpistan. The Canadians have shown a remarkable ability to be good neighbours. Over time, Trimpistan might even begin to emulate some Canadian social and political practises. The proposal also puts Trimp closer to his friends in Russia and North Korea than any other solution." The House exploded in laughter and cheers.

Congressman LaPlante couldn't remain serious any longer. "Madam Chair, colleagues. I'm sorry. I saw this proposal last night on America Speaks and could not resist presenting it. This proposal does not meet the parameters of territory to be ceded to Trimpistan. The territory I have outlined here does not have enough arable land or developed urban area to be considered. I wanted to present it here today so that American citizens could understand that it was presented to our committee and does not meet the parameters of ceded territory set out in the Path to Peace accord. Which is a crying shame, because other than that, it's a beautiful idea." Vermont's congressman bowed and smiled while resuming his seat as 44 of his colleagues cheered and applauded.

Bang! Bang! Bang! Gradually, the House got itself together. AOC was trying hard not to smile. "Having concluded the comedy portion of our proposals, I now ask for serious proposals from the committee that meet the parameters of Article Three, Sub-Section Seven."

After five days of intense emotional deliberation, the committee reached a decision that met the parameters of the Path to Peace Accord.

***

CHAPTER 21.

A Brave New Stan

Michelle Oobima's administration were very busy following the citizenship vote on 31 July 2021. Homeland Security officials were recovering the passport's of the 38 million former American's who chose to 'Leave.' There were multiple new videos each day throughout the summer of famous Trimpistani's having their US passports forcibly taken from them.

On 11 August, Attorney General Sally Bates, escorted by FBI agents, took Trimp's passport from him personally and issued him a tourist's visa. At the same time his secret service security detail was reassigned. An hour after that, DeutscheBank filed to seize any assets associated with Trimp Incorporated.

The IRS responded to DeutscheBank. "The United States Internal Revenue Service seized all Trimp Incorporated assets in 2020 for back taxes owed by the Trimp family. As Donald Trimp is no longer an American citizen you should seek any and all further legal action against Trimp Incorporated through the government of Trimpistan."

"Donald Trimp and the 38 milllion citizen's of Trimpistan are no longer American citizens," Michelle Oobima repeated flatly at a press conference that evening. "Only American citizens are entitled to hold valid United State's passports, so this should not come as a surprise to anyone who voted to 'Leave' the United States. The surrender of US passports by Trimplicans was agreed to in the Path to Peace Accord. Additionally, only former US president's are entitled to security personnel paid for by American taxpayers. By choosing to relinquish his American citizenship Mr. Trimp has also relinquished his right to secret service protection. I also want to remind Americans that the deadline to leave territory being ceded to Trimpistan is 31 Dec of this year. Conversely, Trimplicans must leave the United States by the same date. Questions? Yes, Mr . Hanratty?"

"Madam President, will you accept responsibility if President Trimp is injured without the Secret Service protection he is entitled to?"

"I will not, because citizens of Trimpistan are not entitled to benefits paid for by American taxpayers. If Mr. Trimp is concerned for his safety, he should hire security personnel with his own resources, or have Trimplicans pay for his security. Yes, Diane?

"President Oobima, will citizens of Trimpistan be allowed to hold dual citizenship?"

"Great question. Citizens of Trimpistan could apply to the United States to hold dual citizenship in the future. First, Trimplicans must surrender their American passports and citizenship, and then hold some sort of citizenship in their new country."

"Madam president, when will that citizenship be available to Trimplicans? Where do they apply for citizenship, passports and relocation information?"

"I don't know. That's a great question for anyone connected with the government of Trimpistan," President Oobima replied.

***

On 15 August, President Oobima and Congresswoman Occasional-Cortez outlined Trimpistan's territory at a televised briefing from the Rose Garden. 650 guests were in attendance. The presentation began with an explanation of what parameters had to be met, and why certain areas were chosen over others. The relocation package to aid Americans living in Trimpistan who would be required to leave was also explained.

"This committee was composed of 50 congressmen and congresswomen, one from each state," the president explained. "The committee also included five republican members of congress who voted to 'Leave' America and become citizens of Trimpistan. The committee understood that this secession of territory is emotional, as it requires some 19 million Americans to relocate from territory that will be ceded to Trimpistan. I'm going to have Congresswoman Occasional-Cortez show you the territory that will be ceded to Trimpistan. Congresswoman: thank you for your leadership as chair of this committee."

"Thank you Madam President," AOC began. "I was honored to chair this territorial transition committee. We took our work seriously, and it was incredibly emotional. I will apologise in advance to the 19 million Americans who will need to relocate from designated Trimpistan territory to America. We have programs and funding in place to assist you during this transition. Our committee's final goal was to provide Trimpistan with the amount of land agreed to in the Path to Peace Accord while minimizing the need for Americans and Trimplicans to relocate. We were also careful to ensure that all Indigenous Reservations were not included in Trimpistan territory, but remained in the United States. The ceded territory we agreed on includes wilderness, parts of some National and State Parks, ample arable land for every type of agriculture and suburban and urban areas. The territory we are ceding to Trimpistan does not include any military bases or established state capitols."

The young congresswoman gestured to a screen behind her. "I'll put up the map. What you are seeing here is everyone's first look at Trimpistan." The crowd gasped, then began to applaud.

AOC narrated with a laser pointer in hand. "Trimpistan will be composed of a long narrow band of territory that begins here in southern Montana. It passes through small portions of some heartland states all the way down to northern Florida. Approximately every 100 miles along its length it will narrow to allow for American highways and train tracks to travel east and west across America through Trimpistan. Each crossing point will be monitored by American Border Services Officers augmented by National Guard personnel.

"Cities ceded to Trimpistan will include: Billings Montana, Rapid City South Dakota, Scottsbluff and Omaha Nebraska, Manhattan and Wichita Kansas, Springfield Missouri, Tulsa Oklahoma, Fort Smith Arkansas, Biloxi Mississippi, Mobile Alabama, and Pensacola Florida.

"Americans who live in the area that will become Trimpistan should visit www.transition.usgov as soon as possible to understand what you need to do. We have advisors standing by to help you make this transition to a new place in America as painless as possible. President Oobima, thank you for this opportunity."

"Thank you congresswoman. Next, to explain how this transition will unfold for Trimplicans, I'd like to introduce the vice president of Trimpistan, Ivanka Trimp..." The crowd booed lustily, but President Oobima held up her hands asking for silence. "People. Please. We've had this discussion for some time now. Trimpistan is being formed because we recognise that a nation divided cannot stand. Our differences, perceived and otherwise, were too great to allow us to live in harmony. The Path to Peace recognised that the easiest solution was to allow you, the people, to choose your country. Almost 38 million people chose to 'Leave' America and become citizens of Trimpistan. Americans should want Trimpistan and Trimplicans to succeed. Vice President Trimp. The floor is yours."

Don Jr., Eric and Tiffany applauded half heartedly. It was no secret that both boys had hoped to be vice president. No one was sure what Tiffany hoped to gain from Trimp or Trimpistan, nor if Donald Trimp even recognised Tiffany as his child.

Ivanka's presentation was horrific if you were a proud new citizen of Trimpistan hoping to learn some specific details about your country. For five minutes she showed carefully staged photos of her taken with various world leaders from 2016 to 2019. In each photo, she breathlessly described "here's another picture of me governmenting with world leaders at the International Monetary thingy in 2018..."

"So in conclusion, I want to say that my experiences in governmenting will greatly benefit Trimpistan and Trimplican's for many years to come. Thank you." Ivanka smiled sweetly, expecting applause. The room was awkwardly silent.

"Ms. Trimp, will you be taking any questions from the press?" a NY Times reporter asked, breaking the uncomfortable silence.

"Ummm, sure, I guess," Ivanka replied nervously. "Go ahead."

The journalists all started shouting at once.

"Has the government of Trimpistan laid out a transition plan for Trimpistani's to relocate?"

"Are there going to be elections? Or is your father just seizing the crown of Trimpistan?"

"Will Trimpistan be assisting it's new citizens financially with their relocation from America?"

"When will Trimplican's be able to start moving into Trimpistan?"

"Trimpistani's currently have no citizenship papers. Where should they send their applications?"

Ivanka Trimp was clearly frustrated by the questions. She began to cry. The journalists were still shouting questions as members of Team Trimp hustled her out of the room.

"*GOVERNMENTING IS HARD*" shouted the *NY Times* headline above a photo of the tearful vice president of Trimpistan.

***

CHAPTER 22.

UNEC Resolution 336

Niagara Falls,

On a beautiful crisp October day, the Niagara Regiment were at their spit and polished best. The 500 members who had been deployed as peacekeepers during the Trimp Rebellion had returned home from duty in Florida. The Regiment had lost four members in an IED attack at Mar-A-Lago, and 32 more Niagara's had been wounded.

"Niagara Regiment: A- Ten- Chun!" bellowed their Commanding Officer as the guests of honour arrived in 2 black limousines. 500 gleaming boots rose and fell in unison. The audience in the bleachers applauded and cheered as the Minister of Defence and the Governor General exited the first vehicle. The applause turned to a roar as the young Canadian Prime Minister Elijah and American President Michelle Oobima stepped out of the second limo.

Each of the Niagara's were awarded the UN peacekeeping medal by one of the four guests of honour. Hajit Singh, the Minister of Defence presented medals to Alpha Company. Rock Hansen, Canada's Governor General moved through Bravo Company in his wheelchair. President Oobima gave the 125 soldiers of Charlie Company their medals. Delta Company were presented their medals by Elijah. The Royal Canadian Army Band from CFB Petawawa played while the soldiers received their medals.

The guests of honour reconvened on the dais at the front of the parade square. The soldiers were stood at ease.

"I'm going to keep this short," Elijah promised. The audience cheered. "I just want you all to know how lucky I feel and how extremely proud I am to be Canadian. It is my honour to act as your prime minister. And it is my further honour to welcome the President of the United States, Michelle Oobima, on her first State visit to Canada." The audience rose as one, cheering and applauding. It took several minutes for them to calm down.

Michelle Oobima was clearly touched by this welcome. "Well, thank you for that. Honestly, I'm humbled. As your prime minister did, I will also promise to keep this short. First: let me say that I am incredibly honoured to be here in Canada, and in Niagara Falls. I'm grateful to be given the opportunity to thank the Niagara Regiment personally for their tremendous peacekeeping service to the United

States recently. All Canadians should know that we are eternally grateful for the support Canada has provided to the United States over the last four years. At this time, I'm very proud to make a special presentation to 32 members of the Niagara Regiment who were wounded on their last deployment to the United States."

The master of ceremonies took over the speaking role as President Oobima moved to the front of the dais. "The Canadian Sacrifice Medal is awarded for injuries incurred on deployment. The Sacrifice Medal will be awarded to the following members of the Niagara Regiment...

Corporal Fabiola Gonzalez proudly received her Sacrifice medal wearing her new prosthetic foot. Her fiancé, Master Corporal 'Lumpy' Halerwich lost an eye. Their close friend Corporal 'T-Bone' Brown lost his life.

"Receiving the Sacrifice Medal on behalf of Corporal Brown is his adopted grandmother, Gramma Hanna Halerewich."

The crowd roared its approval as the old lady made her way to the dais. Gramma Hanna was a local legend. Her story as grandmother to a regiment quickly went viral.

***

The Oobima administration working closely with the Canadian government had set a busy schedule for the three day visit to Canada. American security and defence experts met with their Canadian counterparts. The discussion focused on national security from a Canadian and American perspective. There were representatives from both countries military staff along with personnel from the FBI, RCMP, CIA, CSIS, Homeland Security, Border Services and Coast Guards.

Harjit Singh, the Canadian Defence Minister welcomed the group and spoke briefly to the intent of the meeting. "It's good to meet like this again, to share intelligence and strengthen bonds between like minded organizations. We're also hoping for reassurance that Trimpistan won't become a threat to world peace."

Pete Buttedge, the American Secretary of Defense responded. "I want to assure you that no bases, wings, naval stations, military installations, military equipment, arsenals or nuclear weapons are located within the territory granted to Trimpistan." The Canadians looked relieved. An aide brought up a map of the USA with Trimpistan highlighted in red. "In fact, the territory we ceded to Trimpistan looks like it does because we skirted around all our defense establishments. This serves two practical purposes. It gives a mentally unstable leader no readily available weapons that might be used against us or our allies in the near future. Also, as you can see from the map, many of our bases, wings and stations are close to Trimpistan's border, which allows us to maintain secure perimeters and border security while being able to respond quickly to a threat from Trimpistan should that occur. As a final favor to our neighbors, we stopped Trimpistan's border well south of the 49th parallel, and nowhere near the Mexican border. We didn't want Trimpistan's creation or geographic location to pose a problem to Canada or Mexico."

***

Pensacola

Donald Trimp had been busy fund raising since the 'Path to Peace' accord had been ratified. He got busier after 1 August when the territorial border of Trimpistan was made public. He held numerous hate rallies (with a $90.00 ticket cost) in Trimpistan territory in which the recurring theme was: "America is lost. Forget those losers. Trimpistan will be far greater than America ever was, trust me. But first, we need your help. We need to purchase or build regional capitol buildings, schools for our children, factories for our industries..."

Crowds at the rallies dwindled once word got out that Trimp and Trimpistan needed money.

19 million Americans needed to leave the territory ceded to Trimpistan and relocate in the USA no later than 31

December 2021. Most began to leave Trimpistan in early August, after the territorial borders were established.

Twenty million Trimplicans already lived within the territory ceded to Trimpistan. The territorial transition committee had done a good job on this. As directed they had chosen the territory to be ceded considering the least possible disruption to Americans and Trimplicans.

Trimplicans outside of Trimpistan seemed less keen to relocate than their American cousins. Eighteen million Trimplicans, or approximately 45 % of their population, had yet to move into their new country by October 2021.

'The Stone' reminded Trimplicans that the vote to 'Leave' was not reversible. "Don't forget that you here are on a tourist visa in America. If I were you, I would not wait to get to Trimpistan. I hear it's going to be a paradise, heaven on earth."

Trimplicans were starting to complain that Trimpistan was not ready to receive them.

"There's no schools, no police, the hospitals aren't staffed."

"I heard the power company shut down, and the municipal workers in the town we're moving to all left."

"I keep calling Trimpistan government service numbers, but no one picks up. Can you help?"

The response from the American transition team volunteers and employees was firm, fair and consistent.

"I'm sorry to hear this, but we can't help you. We're the transition team for Americans leaving Trimpistan. You should go to Trimpistan and solve your problems there in person. I'm sure Donald Trimp will hire the very best people to help you."

Property values in Trimpistan were dropping one or two percentage points per day. Property values more than fifty miles outside Trimpistan were climbing. (American buyers seemed reluctant to live near Trimpistan, unless they had Trimplican relatives or friends they still spoke to, but this was rare.) Trimpanzees selling property in America and relocating to Trimpistan were getting the best short term deal: they were benefitting twice by selling at good prices in America and buying at lower prices in Trimpistan. Trimp and his children (who were essentially the entire appointed government of Trimpistan) boasted about this win - win scenario nonstop on Parler and Facebook. Twitter had removed all the Trimp family for repeated ethical violations in 2020.

Michelle Oobima's administration set up relief payments and a variety of services for relocating Americans as promised by the transition team. Vice President Dwain John-Stone was the leader of the transition team. The Stone was everywhere at once. He encouraged people to help relocating Americans. He was ladling soup at shelters, helping unload moving trucks, painting, setting up welcoming committees...

Many relocating Americans had already sold at a loss to Trimpanzees and purchased new homes at inflated prices. In those cases, the American government looked at the previous year's assessment values and reimbursed the homeowner their losses. Other Americans needed financial help until they could find work. Americans who could help were housing people or families during relocation. Arenas, public buildings and schools were set up as temporary shelters for those in transit. By the end of December 2021 98% of Americans who needed to relocate, some 18.9 million souls, had vacated Trimpistan. 100,000 people had applied to remain in Trimpistan, or submitted a post election 'Leave' vote.

Beginning on 1 December 2021, the American Armed Forces worked cooperatively with Homeland Security Officers, State troopers, American Border Patrol personnel and Immigrations and Customs Enforcement officers to relocate the remaining 11 eleven million Trimplicans from America to their new country. Fifty percent of those relocating went grumbling or shouting. The remainder had to be arrested, physically restrained and delivered to the nearest Trimpistan / American border station. The Trimpistan side of the border wasn't being monitored or staffed. Essentially the Trimplicans were processed by the American side, their tourist visas were rescinded and then they were pushed through the gates into Trimpistan. By 29 December, the relocation portion of the Path to Peace resolution was complete. Seventy six American security personnel were killed and ninety four Trimplicans died during the relocation phase in December.

***

Geneva, United Nations Environmental Council
7 July 2022

UNEC Resolution 336: Be it resolved that the Plaintiffs (United States, Canada and Mexico) have registered formal complaints against Trimpistan for poor environmental practises. The specific environmental complaints against Trimpistan (the Defendant) are:

- i): Overfishing / Illegal Harvesting in the Gulf of Mexico;
- ii): Raw Sewage / Industrial Pollution in the Gulf of Mexico;
- iii): Groundwater/Freshwater Pollution, Great Plains Aquifer and related Tributaries;
- iv): Heavy Metal Pollution / Mining violations;

vi): Forestry / Clear cutting Violations;

vii): Protected Species Violations;

viii): C02 / Methane Release Violations;

ix): Nuclear Waste Handling Violations;

x): Pesticide / Insecticide Release Violations; and

ix): Faecal Sludge Application Violations.

The Defendant is hereby advised that these formal complaints will be heard in UNEC beginning 17 August 2022.

Trimpistan's response to the Council was short and abrupt and delivered by Parler, the popular social media platform for right wingers. Eric Trimp, Secretary of Environment and Agriculture filmed himself opening, reading and urinating on the letter. "Trimplicans are free men. We do not recognise any government or authority outside our borders," was the printed response under the video.

***

21 October 2022

1. Re UNEC Resolution 336. Be advised that UNEC has heard the complaints against Trimpistan and sided with the Plaintiffs. The 186 members of UNEC voted unanimously to impose trade

sanctions on the purchase of the following products and resources originating in Trimpistan:

- i) fish, shellfish and fish by product;
- ii) timber and pulp product;
- iii) agricultural product including meats, grains, legumes, fruits, vegetables and textiles;
- iv) manufactured goods of metal, plastic or wood;
- v) weapons;
- vi) pharmaceuticals and medical equipment;
- vii) water;
- viii) metals, and
- ix) petroleum or solid fuel products including coal and wood.

2. Be advised that further environmental complaints to this council will result in more trade sanctions.

***

CHAPTER 23.

The People's Army

7 Jan 2029

Washington

Outgoing President Michelle Oobima was guiding her administration through the turnover to the incoming president and her staff. At 39, Alexandria Ocassional-Cortez was by far the youngest president-elect in American history, and the first Latina. She had become the environmental champion of the Oobima Administration through her relentless work on the Green New Deal.

Historians generally agreed that the Green New Deal would have been a tough sell had the United States not allowed Trimpistan to secede. "Trimp's cult members would have fought the Green New Deal tooth and nail," stated a Harvard political science professor. "'It's very likely that they would have killed President Oobima, the president-elect, and anyone else who supported this project." The same historians and scholars mostly agreed that the Path to Peace Accord had achieved its goals.

The United States had made good progress from a socio-economic standpoint following Trimpistan's secession. American's had one of the best medicare systems in the world: it served all Americans, not just the wealthy. The tax code had been blown up and rebuilt in 2021, allowing the US to begin repayment of staggering national debt. Michelle Oobima's administration had recorded six successive deficit budgets. The Independent government had reinvested public money in education and infrastructure. They had subsidized the use of renewable energy, and reduced reliance on fossil fuels without crippling their economy. In fact, the transformation from gas and oil to renewable energy was one of America's major economic drivers.

The fledgling American Conservative Party had done well in the 2028 election. Following the secession of Trimpistan in 2022, the Republican Party crumpled, imploded and ceased to exist. "You can't wash the stench and stain of Trimp and Trimp supporters off that party name," said their new leader Bryan Wright. "Please don't think of us as a rebranded or renamed GOP. Very few real conservatives were loyal to Trimp or the Republican party after 2016. The ACP attracted many voters and some Independent Party politicians who believed that America needed a conservative voice.

Michelle Oobima didn't see the Conservative Party as problematic. "A healthy democracy needs healthy debate with voices from the left, centre and right side of the political spectrum."

The Democratic Party had become the centre of that spectrum. Most Independent Party politicians were left of centre.

***

Pensacola, Trimpistan Capitol

"In our lead story tonight, President Trimp of Trimpistan has been arrested and overthrown by a citizen's militia in that nation's capitol. We warn our viewers that some of these images will be disturbing."

"We, the People's Army have placed the Trimp family under arrest for crimes against the people of Trimpistan," said a young masked spokeswoman. The people behind the young lady speaking looked angry, hungry and feral.

"My name is Sarah Sullivan. I've been appointed as the spokesperson for the People's Army. Trimp and his spawn lied to our parents. They tax Trimpistanis brutally, and give us nothing in return. Our people are starving. There are no schools and very few doctors. Our water is not fit to drink, it's been poisoned by unsafe fracking. We have no jobs. Trimpistan has never held fair and free elections. Our governors, judges and police have all been appointed by

Trimp. Those people have all the food and all the money. They live in nice warm homes while we starve in the cold. They have used their absolute power viciously to keep us down. We, the young people of Trimpistan, will not stand for this. It ends now."

The camera panned across a dystopian landscape. Pensacola was a ruined ghetto. Decaying buildings, garbage everywhere, burning cars. Those who had visited the outer regions in central and north Trimpistan said it was worse there.

"Over the coming days, we will elect a new government. Until then, the country formerly known as Trimpistan will be ruled by our People's Army. Pray for us if you believe in that sort of thing. Our elders did, and believed that God chose Trimp to lead us to a Promised Land. Look around. How's that working out for us? Anyway, if you're watching this, I'm one of the few drones that has a working phone. 88-676-012."

***

Ottawa.

Elijah and many of the original members of the Independent People's Party were retired from politics. One of the 'Indie's' original ideas was that people should not view elected office as a lifelong job, that there should instead be term limits. In the last Canadian federal election, the leader of the IPP, KT Burfitt was selected as prime minister. KT was a former journalist, and a former elder of the Simpleton Commune in BC. She was a single mother of an adopted daughter named Susanna. She and Susanna had just seen the piece on the rebellion in Trimpistan.

KT reached for her phone. "Can I speak to Sarah Sullivan please?"

***

Postface

I hope you enjoyed reading the Mouse and Elephant trilogy as much as I enjoyed writing it. I have received some great feedback via social / anti-social media from people who loved or hated the series.

To the people who loved the books, thank you. Many of you appreciated the fact that the goal of satirical fiction is to serve as a warning. To do this, I had to make some predictions set in the near future. Some of my predictions - especially the hopeful predictions about environmental progress - were ridiculously optimistic. If I'm gonna dream, I might as well dream big. Am I more of an optimist than a realist? Yes. I'll keep hoping.

On the flip side, many of you initially wondered if my criticism of Trimp and the Trimpanzees wasn't overly harsh or cruel. *"He's not that crazy,"* or *"Trust democracy: the checks and balances in their system won't let that happen."* Again, I was dreaming big. I didn't wanna be right. Am I more of a pessimist than a realist? No.

To the many Trimp supporters who contacted me through anti-social media, thank you. Some of your comments were delightfully hilarious and helpful. I like to think most people can be saved. I don't like to think that 74 million of my neighbours are inherently evil. If there's any doubt in your mind, if you think your loyalty to Cult 45 may have been a mistake, you might want to study German history from 1918 through to present day. The key lessons to consider would include:

i)   how to recognise fascism- 1918-1945;

ii) how to distance yourself from ever having supported a fascist dictator- 1945-1947, and

iii) how a national education strategy plays a vital role in admitting that you had a fascist dictator and that fascist dictators are bad.

Unless of course you believe that fascist dictators are good. If this last sentence applies to you, I'm afraid you are beyond help. Just know I'll always oppose your goals.

Always and always,

Mark Piper

www.ingramcontent.com/pod-product-compliance
Lightning Source LLC
Chambersburg PA
CBHW020303200626
46814CB00006BA/2064